MARTHA KARPOFF

Park Hae Jin DOES THE

KAMA SUTRA

OR THE SWEETEST STORY EVER TOLD

Park Hae Jin Does the Kama Sutra or the Sweetest Story Ever Told

Martha Karpoff

Kravitz and Sons LLC
204 E Arlington Blvd. Suite B
Greenville, NC 27858

Published by Kravitz and Sons LLC.

ISBN: 979-8-89639-558-4 (sc)
ISBN: 979-8-89639-559-1 (e)

Table of Contents

Chapter 1
Kidnapped!

I landed in the airport at Incheon after leaving the U.S. on my way to Malaysia. As I was entering the station, there was a disturbance right before me. A bunch of guys swarmed over me and a taller guy who was near me. Suddenly, I was grabbed and dragged to a van as was the tall guy. I heard someone say, "Who's she?" and "Just bring her."

I woke up on a mattress in a fairly small rectangular room. I really needed to go to the bathroom. Sitting up, I saw a nice-looking Korean man across the room, staring, or should I say glaring, at me. I glanced the other way; there was a wall that jutted out into the room and what appeared to be a shower. Assuming that it was the bathroom, I hurried over, and despite having no door, at least the wall blocked the view. I gratefully emptied my bladder. There was a sink and some soap, so I washed my hands and face.

Walking into the room, the guy jumped up, grabbed my arm, and said something in Korean. He seemed angry. I looked up into his eyes and saw that it was none other than Park Hae Jin!

"I'm sorry, but I don't speak Korean well. Do you speak some English?" I asked.

"Who the hell are you?" he yelled, "What are you doing to me?"

"I'm just a regular person from the U.S., but you look like the actor Park Hae Jin. Are you his stunt double or something?"

"How do you know me?"

"I've watched some Korean shows on Netflix. Are you really Park Hae Jin?"

Releasing my arm, Mr. Park nearly pushed me to the ground.

"Calm down," I said. "What's going on here? Where are we?" Glancing around the room, I said, "Where's the door?"

I approached the walls, which seemed to be covered in cloth, and looked for the door out of the room. I ran my hands over the walls. There did seem to be some seams. I carefully tried to slip my fingers into the seams to see if there was an opening.

When I was about halfway around the room, Mr. Park said, "I've already tried."

"Let me look again, then." I continued and found nothing. The only other features in the room included a minibar on the wall that defined the bathroom. It included a small sink, a microwave, and a refrigerator. I looked in the cabinet under the sink, but it didn't seem as though there was any way to come or go out under the sink.

I looked at the room; the only other feature was the mattress on the floor. "Have you looked under the mattress?" I asked him.

He stood up and went to the mattress. Together, we flipped it over. Nothing.

"Let's examine the floor."

We walked around the floor, at times getting on our hands and knees.

I lay down on the mattress. "Come here, and let's look at the ceiling." Mr. Park complied fairly quickly, and we began to examine the ceiling. It was unusually high. There were inset lights and possibly some panels that could be opened. Since the wall separating the room from the bathroom was only a half-wall in height, it would be impossible to reach the ceiling by standing on the wall.

"Well, this is quite a quandary," I said.

"What does quandary mean?" asked Mr. Park.

"A problem or a puzzle."

I stood up and went over and sat by a wall. He sat across the room (which wasn't too far) against the opposite wall.

"Okay, who are you?" he asked.

"My name is Martha Karr, and I'm from the United States. I have an acquaintance in Seoul I was going to visit."

"That's it?" he said.

"What else would be helpful? I'm not someone rich or famous. Whatever's going on here is not about me."

"So... it's about me?"

"I would think so.... Is this some sort of PR stunt?"

"No."

"Maybe not that you're involved in, but maybe from your agent or agency?"

This time, he stopped for a while and seemed to be thinking about it.

"No."

"Does someone have a grudge against you? Or do you have fans who would do this?"

"Why would they?" he shot back.

"I don't know, but this seems like a pretty pricey operation to kidnap us and put us in a seemingly escape-proof room."

"Why are you here then?" he asked.

"Maybe I'm just a mistake. Maybe I was near you at the airport or got in the way. I don't know!"

Both of us went into our respective sulks.

I went to the fridge and found some bottled water.

"You want one?" I asked.

He nodded, and I handed it to him. Then, I went back to my side of the room.

"Have you had any arguments with anyone lately?" I asked.

"No."

We were back to one-word answers.

"Tell me more about you. Maybe there's some connection," he asked.

"My husband and friend of 50 years died last year. I'm 75 years old and have a small savings account and Social Security."

"What!?" he exclaimed. "You don't seem that old."

I smiled, "Well, thank you, I think."

He looked dumbfounded,

"When we were younger, we (my husband and I) participated in community development projects in the Philippines, Indonesia, and Malaysia. I know a few people in these countries, and I'm moving to Malaysia."

"You're 75 years old?"

"Yes. Is that all you got out of my talk?"

I blinked my eyes a few times and ran my hand through my hair. I took a big swig of water. Park Hae Jin finished his.

"Okay, Sherlock. Did you ascertain or see any connection?" I asked.

Mr. Park didn't answer, and I noticed his eyes were closing, and he was lurching to the side. I ran over and propped him up. Sitting down next to him while holding him up, I suddenly felt sleepy, too, and felt myself leaning on him. I fell asleep.

I woke up to find myself on the floor near the wall. Mr. Park was also on the floor, a little further down the wall. I pushed myself up and hurried back to the bathroom. After using the toilet, I got a wash rag and went to Mr. Park. I wiped his hands and face, and he gradually woke up. I helped him get up and took him to the toilet. I told him to pee and wash up. I looked at the water bottles. He had completely emptied his, while mine was only half empty. He staggered out of the bathroom, and I helped him to the mattress.

"Try not to fall asleep again. I'll rinse out your bottle and give you some water from the faucet. I think 'they' put something in the water."

He shook his head from side to side.

As I was over at the minibar, I noticed a plate of sandwiches. I rinsed out both of our water bottles and put some water in both. I took the bottles to the mattress, knelt before him, and helped him drink some water. I drank some, too, as I was thirsty after our drugged sleep.

"Look, Mr. Park, there are some sandwiches over there, but if 'they' can drug the water, 'they' can drug the food, too. I'm not sure if we should eat anything. The alternative is to wait until we're really tired and then eat something."

He still seemed groggy, so I had him stand up and walked him around the room a few times. Finally, he shook me off and staggered around on his own.

"Well, at least we know they have a way to get in and out of here since they left these sandwiches," I said.

"What's your name again?" he asked.

"It's Martha."

"Why don't we sit and talk again, Martha?"

"Okay, but we probably need to sit close together, as 'they' may be listening to us."

Once we had arranged ourselves where we thought best, he quietly asked if I thought we were in danger.

"Since 'they' took us by force and have probably drugged us at least twice and have held us in an inescapable room, I would say we're already experiencing danger or at least a threat of some kind. My main questions are: how long do they plan to hold us and what is their end game? Will they just let us go, or will they kill us?"

"I agree. This is very extreme. They've put themselves in danger in a way. They have to maintain their anonymity," he said.

"I think our first concern is if they are going to let us go right away, like tomorrow or the next day. If they do, great, but if they don't, we need to decide ways or activities to survive."

"If they kill us quickly, I guess our problem is solved," he said.

"The effort they've put into this set-up makes me think they're in it for the long haul. Why? Are you so wealthy that someone could make a bundle through a ransom?"

"Maybe my lawyer's family and agency could come up with a couple of million dollars-but that's about it."

I reached out and grabbed his hand. We looked at each other for a while. Finally, I smiled and said, "You really are a handsome guy." He laughed.

"Look, this situation has made us instant friends and confidants. I think they didn't intend for me to be here. I think they wanted to drive you crazy or torture you. I'm perfectly able to do that to you myself, so maybe they'll leave the task to me."

He pushed me away, and I laughed a lot.

"Are you in on this?" he asked, climbing over me and holding my arms to the floor. "Well, are you?"

"I'm sorry. I have a weird sense of humor. I just suddenly found the whole thing funny. I'm not in on anything against you."

Chapter 2
Fear-Filled Imprisonment

He got up and started pacing.

"That's a good plan. Why don't you do a bunch of exercises-which I'm sure you're good at-while I shower? After that, we'll eat our own potentially poisoned sandwiches, go to bed, and get some sleep," I said.

I went to the bathroom, took off my clothes, and stepped into the shower. Because of the openness of the bathroom, the shower was fully visible from the main room. I said, "What the hell?" to myself and proceeded. After I finished, I went to the sink, washed out my panties and bra, and hung them up on a towel rack. I put my shirt and jeans back on and went into the bedroom. Mr. Park was doing pushups.

"Good man," I said. "The shower's free now. I always say, 'Taking a shower can change the course of your whole day.' I'll wait for you to eat."

After he came back, we looked at the sandwiches.

"I am hungry, but this food might have a sleeping potion or perhaps even poison," I said.

"It seems like if they were going to kill us, they would have already done so," he replied.

"Well, I don't think I will necessarily be afforded the protection you may have." I looked at the ceiling and yelled, "I'm really good at sleeping, so you don't have to drug me!"

Addressing Mr. Park, I said, "Could you yell that up to the ceiling in Korean? These people probably don't speak English."

He laughed but eventually complied. "Are we going to eat?"

"I think it would be best if you didn't, at least for tonight. I'll take a couple of bites, and you can observe me. Since I'm so much older than you and I'm not anyone special, I'm willing to sacrifice myself in the hopes that you can come out of this intact."

"What crazy stuff are you saying?"

"I'm saying something seriously weird is going on here, and we may not make it. If one has to go first, I'll do it. I've had a great life until now; I was married to a wonderful man for 45 years, met many people from all over the world, and lived in relative comfort."

I reached over, took two bites of a sandwich, and drank my water.

"Tomorrow, we can re-evaluate."

I threw the rest of the sandwiches in the trash, went to the bathroom, came back, and lay myself down on the mattress.

"I'm going to sleep. Once I decide to sleep, I go to sleep quickly. I think you should sleep next to me just to stay warm and for defensive purposes. I sleep on my side so you can put your back to mine. Since one or both of us may not wake up, I think we should say something significant before we sleep."

"What do you mean, significant?"

"Well, something that congratulates us on making it through the day and projects that we'll have another day together tomorrow. I was thinking of a lullaby or something a parent or older brother or sister might say. Do you know anything?"

Mr. Park just looked stunned.

"In my house when I was a kid there was one saying, 'Don't let the bedbugs bite'."

"Did you have bedbugs at your house?" asked Mr. Park.

"No. It was just a funny saying to dismiss kids from the living room into their beds. Another thing I thought of was a baby's lullaby. It went something like this,

> *Lullaby and good night*
> *On this soft evening light*
> *So farewell, evening friend*
> *'Til we waken again.*

"I like that: 'Farewell friend, 'til we waken again.' What do you think?"

"Who and what the hell are you?"

"I'm tired. Farewell, friend, 'til we waken again."

I could hear him moving around for a while, and then I fell asleep.

When I awoke, I could feel him behind my back. The room was fully illuminated as it was last night. I walked quickly to the bathroom, did my business, and put my dry bra and panties back on.

Going into the kitchen area, I saw a couple of ramen noodle bowls on the counter. The wastebasket had been cleared of the sandwiches I put in last night. There was a little post-it note on the counter, but it was in Korean, so I couldn't read it. I retrieved my water bottle, filled it, and went to sit by a wall. I looked at Mr. Park for a while and thought about how truly pretty he was. I dozed off again while sitting there.

Suddenly, somebody was kicking my leg. "Hey!" I yelled and sat up. Mr. Park jumped back about three feet.

"I was just checking if you were alive."

He looked startled and contrite at the same time.

"Yeah. It looks like we made it. Although we're going to have trouble telling how much time has passed if this keeps up."

"There was a note with the food in the kitchen. It said there will be no drugs in the food or water from now on."

"Too bad I can't read Korean. Let's eat!"

After microwaving our ramen bowls, we sat down on the floor to eat. They had left some wooden chopsticks. Of course, I had never eaten ramen with chopsticks, or really anything with chopsticks-though I had tried several times in the past. Mr. Park watched me for several minutes while I fruitlessly tried my best. He smiled. He raised an eyebrow.

"Yes, I am incompetent. Just illustrate with your hands how to do it."

I watched. I tried a few times. I failed. He laughed his head off.

I decided to drink the broth and eat the noodles with my fingers. It worked pretty well.

After washing my hands, I came out of the bathroom and sat down.

"It seems as though they can hear us," I said.

"Yes, and they responded positively."

"Did they mention anything about how long we would be here?" I asked.

"No."

"Maybe we should shout a few questions or requests at them every day and see what we get."

"Good idea. We need to make a list," he said. Suddenly, he yelled something in Korean at the ceiling. "I just asked them for pencil and paper or maybe some chalk to write on the walls."

We both stared at the ceiling for a while, but nothing happened.

"Okey-dokey. Let's think about what we should do today. You look as though you work out a lot-so we could do that. You work out, and I'll try to copy you. Any other ideas?"

"I could give you another chopsticks lesson," said Mr. Park.

"I can give you English lessons and maybe some U.S. history lessons.... Maybe not all today, though."

"I could teach you Korean."

"We could sing songs, dance around, and take naps."

"That's enough of a list for now. I'll do my exercise routine."

"Me too!" I shouted as I hopped up.

He began with some pushups. I bent over as far as I could and back up a few times until I got tired.

He did some deep squats with his hands out in front of him. I stretched my arms over my head.

"Are you sure you're copying me?" he asked.

"Everyone sees things differently," I murmured.

"I'm going to do some laps around the room. Let's move the mattress to the middle," he said.

So, I got up and started to run laps, too. After one lap, he passed me. I kept slogging away and eventually did four laps while he did twelve. I flopped down on the mattress while he continued his personal journey. Pretty soon, the whole room smelled like a gym. In other words, the famous actor stank to high heaven. Sweat poured down his head and his t-shirt. He looked good in his wet t-shirt.

After he stopped, I said, "Okay, stinky, go take a shower and be sure to wash your clothes out with soap. You can put on a towel for a while."

"Maybe we should ask for detergent," I said to myself.

I went over to the minibar because, even though I so wanted to see him take a shower, from here, I could avoid the view. I sat there, trying to control my crazy thoughts. Eventually, he came out with his towel on.

"Why are you cowering in the corner?" he asked.

"I tend to do that," I said.

"What?"

"Forget it," I said. "Let's drink some water."

We drank a bunch of water. After that, I went to the bathroom, grabbed the other towel, gave it to him, and said, "Please drape this over your shoulders, (his chest was extremely distracting) and then let's brainstorm the things we need."

He looked puzzled. "Okay."

Sitting down, I said, "Just yell up to the ceiling in Korean after each thing I say, and then you can yell up any other requests you can think of. One-bath robes; two-a couple of sweat suits. (We could use them as pajamas.)" He yelled to the ceiling after every request. "Some socks and panties." "A couple of new toothbrushes-because I'm tired of using yours...."

Mr. Park suddenly jumped up and shouted, "You've been using my toothbrush?"

"What did you think? I would just let my teeth fall out of my head?"

"This is totally unacceptable!" He threw the towel around his neck (that I had just talked him into putting on) onto the floor.

"Look, my husband and I accidentally used each other's toothbrushes on several occasions, and we were perfectly fine."

Mr. Park suddenly screamed something at the ceiling, which I assumed was demanding a shitload of toothbrushes. "Get out of my sight!"

I looked around, trying to figure out where I could go to do that. The only place was the toilet. "Oh well," I thought after drinking all that water. I killed two birds with one stone.

Thinking I might not have a chance to brush my teeth again if he got a hold of the toothbrush, I put some toothpaste on it and yelled, "Na na, na na, na na—I'm brushing my teeth."

And suddenly, a clatter arose from the bedroom. Mr. Park came around the corner yelling, "No--???!"

He grabbed my hand and lifted it away from my mouth.

"Drop it," he said.

Chapter 3
Exploring Boundaries

"Two can play this game," I said as I put my other hand down on the towel that was around his waist. He shook my arm until I dropped the toothbrush, which fell into the toilet. We both stared at the toilet for a few seconds. With my other hand still on the towel, I stepped forward and pushed him against the wall near the shower. My thoughts were not good. Staring intently at each other, I finally dropped my eyes and stepped back, releasing my hand from the towel.

"Okay, let's calm down a minute," I said.

"You're right. We shouldn't fight over a toothbrush."

"You grab the shampoo out of the shower, and I'll get the toothbrush out of the toilet."

Meeting at the sink, he said, "Are we actually going to use this after dropping it in the toilet?" he asked.

"Let's think about that later."

I rinsed off the toothpaste in the sink, put some shampoo on the toothbrush, and massaged it thoroughly. I rinsed it and repeated the process.

"Go in the kitchen and heat up a cup of water. We'll pour it over the brush-and please don't burn yourself in the process."

He returned shortly with the cup of water, and slowly poured it over the brush which I held over the sink. After giving it one final knockout on the sink, I put it in the little rack for toothbrushes by the sink.

"Okay, let's let it air dry," I said.

We walked back into the bedroom. He returned the cup to the small kitchen counter.

For some reason, we found ourselves holding hands and sat down on the floor with our backs to the mattress.

After sitting there for a while, we let go of each other's hands and put them on our laps.

"I am sorry for riling you up like that," I said while staring at the floor.

"I am sorry for grabbing your arm."

"Sitting here next to you like this reminds me of a scene from a K-drama."

"You watch K-dramas?"

"I already told you that. I watched them all the time, but only on Netflix because that's basically all I had access to. We didn't have a big budget, so we limited ourselves in the number of services we subscribed to."

"By 'we', you mean you and your husband."

"Yeah, Ian."

"Did Ian like K-dramas, too?"

"Some he liked. But mostly, he thought I watched too many handsome Korean men too often. He seemed irritated at times.

"Anyway, back to the scene I was talking about," I continued. "It's in *Something in the Rain*. The two protagonists are Jin-a and Jun-hui. Did I pronounce those right?"

"Close enough. I've seen the show before, so continue."

"These two have been wanting to become boyfriend and girlfriend, but it seems as though their timing is always off. They are sitting at a table in a bar with some of his co-workers and one of her co-workers who is also interested in Jun-hui. The male co-workers are grilling Jun-hui and bragging about how many girlfriends he had in the army. The woman from Jin-a's office pipes up and says something like, 'So you have a 100% success rate with women?' And he says, 'More like 99%.'

"Well, that drives the whole table of co-workers wild. They ask him why only 99%, and he admits he's never asked the girl he's thinking about out.

"Around this time, Jin-a reaches over (while drinking a beer) under the table and takes his hand. Immediately, Jun-hui gets the hiccups. Then Jun-hui interlaces or entwines their fingers on that hand, and Jin-a gets the hiccups. Someone in the group asks, 'Are hiccups contagious?'"

I jump up and say, "Let's get our water bottles. These will be our beer bottles."

Sitting back down beside him, I say, "Okay, let's start pretending."

I looked at Mr. Park and said, "So, you are saying that you have a 100% success rate with women?"

Mr. Park looked at me and said, "More like 99%, because I never asked her."

I sipped my water and tried to grab his hand, but I only got a handful of towels. I looked down and said, "Where's your fucking hand?"

"Oh, is it supposed to be down here near your leg?"

"Yes, I'm sorry I didn't explain it enough." So, grabbing his hand, I placed it where I thought it should be. "Let's start over."

"Are you saying you have a 100% success rate with women?"

He said, "Yes," and grabbed my hand.

"You just can't follow directions, can you? How did you ever make it in show business?"

"I want to see your hiccups," he said, staring straight at me while smiling dangerously.

"We both want to see things in this life," I say, staring at the towel on the lower half of his body.

"Hiccups," he says as he squeezed my hand a little tighter.

"Okay, okay!" I sort of gave a squeak in my throat while raising my shoulders up and down. I fluttered my eyelids at him.

He burst into a profound laughter. "Worst hiccups I've ever seen."

I pried my hand out of his and stood by a wall as far away as possible. "Why don't you go see if your clothes are dry by now?" I asked.

"Good idea," he said. Over the wall, he said, "The underwear is almost dry. I'll put them on."

I felt relieved. He rounded the corner and stood before me. The t-shirt and briefs were still quite wet, and the contours underneath were well-defined. I pursed my lips.

"You call that dry?" I asked. "Go back to your towels otherwise, you might catch a cold."

Suddenly, laughter rang out from the ceiling. A voice said something in Korean, and then in English! "You two are hilarious. Now move to the bathroom because we're going to drop some things down to you in the bedroom."

As we crossed over to the bathroom, I said to Mr. Park, "You just keep your back to me." More laughter from the ceiling.

I pushed Mr. Park toward the sink and toilet. "Your backside is almost as disturbing as the front. Please put a towel around you now!"

Just then, a big "plop" came from the bedroom as a large trash bag full of stuff fell from the ceiling. Glancing upward, we also saw a medium-sized box descending via some cords. Once the box hit the floor, two cords that were supporting the box were pulled up. The ceiling then closed up.

Mr. Park tied a towel around his waist, and we peeked into the bedroom. "I don't hear any ticking sounds, but let's check the box first." The faint sound of laughter drifted down.

The box held foodstuffs, including a small rice cooker and a bag of rice. There were several containers of fresh sides and a nice stew in one container.

"Wow, they are even cooking for us," I said.

Mr. Park went over to the plastic bag and dumped it on the floor. There were a couple of sweatsuits, additional underwear and socks, two more towels, and two new toothbrushes.

"They are fulfilling our every wish," I said.

After splitting up our goods into my pile and his pile, I said, "Please go change into some dry clothes before you get sick."

Mr. Park jumped up, taking the clothes he needed, and came back fully dressed.

"Do you want some rice?" I asked.

We put some rice and water in the cooker, plugged it in, and pushed the start button. I noticed the controls were all in Korean.

After eating and cleaning up, I pulled Mr. Park over to the bed and quietly said, "Let's have a quick talk." And a little more loudly, "We need a nap."

Laying down facing each other, I said, "Look, Mr. Park, just because they treated us nicely doesn't mean they're our friends or even if they are friendly toward us, it doesn't mean their boss or bosses are. We should enjoy whatever we can here and keep a positive attitude yet be constantly alert. I am concerned about them separating us through some trick. If they take me, saying they are going to let me go because I'm an innocent bystander, they could easily kill me, and you'd never know. I would certainly raise an alarm about you with the police, although I wouldn't know where you were."

Mr. Park took up the story, "And if they take me, who knows what they'll do to me or to you. Maybe they'd remove me to another place, and a couple of weeks later, they'll let you go. My trail is cold."

By this time, we were holding hands as we talked.

"A likely outcome is they kill us, either separately or together," I said.

After a long pause, I said, "I suddenly feel sleepy."

"You don't think they drugged us again, do you?" said Mr. Park as his eyes closed....

Much later, I woke up in his arms with my back facing his front. This was different from our back-to-back sleeping habits. One of his hands was under me and clamped nicely on one of my breasts. I thought to myself, "This isn't half bad." And, also, "How do I get out of this without waking him up?"

I put my hand on his and slowly extracted myself from his grasp, wiggling forward and falling off the mattress at the end of my journey, only making a slight thud-like sound.

He bolted upright and said, "Martha!"

I rolled over and sat up, "Don't worry. Here I am."

We stared bleary-eyed at each other.

"Seems like it's exercise time. I'm going to the bathroom."

After washing my face and combing my hair, I came back to find him sitting there, slumped over, his hair dangling cutely.

"Up, Mr. Park. Let's see how sweaty and stinky you can become today."

He threw his head back and glared mightily at me, stumbled to his feet, and into the bathroom. I pushed the mattress to the middle of the floor on my hands and knees. I started doing some bend-overs and stretched my arms up over my head. He joined me in this enterprise but did a much better job. Soon, we started our little jog around the mattress. I made it around six times today but felt pretty dizzy and breathless. Sitting in the bathroom doorway/opening, I watched as he continued. When he got to pushups, squats, and jumping jacks, I joined back in for a couple of minutes. Finally, he started stripping off his clothes on the way to the shower.

"You've successfully stunk up the place! Please wash yourself and your clothes thoroughly."

He came out later with his sweatpants on. I took a shower and washed my clothes, too. Then, I put on the tracksuit and returned to the bedroom.

"We need to request some more stuff from the crowd up above. I want a small bag of crunchy Cheetos. I also wonder if they could turn off the lights at night-time, so we could know that time is passing. I need some extra virgin coconut oil for my skin."

"It would be nice if we knew the date and time," said Mr. Park. He began to state our requests in Korean to the gods up above.

Chapter 4
Starting Classes

"What if we start our classes to pass the time? I'll tell you some things about grade school in American schools. Of course, I went to school in the fifties."

"What if I already know the stuff?" he asked.

"Just tell me, and I'll skip that and go on to something else.

"So, let's start with the ABC song. Do you know it?"

"I don't think so. What do you mean by the fifties?"

"The 1950's," I say.

He gasped and appeared to be doing some mental calculations. "Wow."

"I'll start singing the ABC song, but I think I forgot the ending. Do you know it?"

"No."

"Okay, then. Sing it with me. ABCDEFG. Sing that part with me."

"Good. The next part is HIJKLMNOP. Let's try it."

"HIJKLMNOP," together.

"QRS and TUV. This has an 'and' in it for the rhythm of the song. Let's go again."

"QRS and TUV."

"W and XYZ," I sang.

He sang "W and XYZ."

"Now we know our ABC's blah, blah, blah, blah, blah, blah, blah. I forgot the ending and I may have written the letters wrong, too. Okay, let's try the whole thing together:

"ABCDEFGHIJKLMNOP, QRS and TUV, W and XYZ. Now we know our ABC's, blah, blah, blah, blah, blah, blah."

We both laughed, and Mr. Park said, "I like the blah blah part the best."

We went around singing blah, blah…for quite a while and laughing. After the laughter died down, I said, "That reminds me of another children's song: Baa, Baa, Black Sheep." I sang:

"Baa, Baa, Black sheep,
Have you any wool?
Yes sir. Yes, sir. Three bags full.
One for my master,
One for the dame and

But I might amend it and say, 'one for the pretty boy who lives in the lane."

Why thank you, Martha."

"Let's sing it together."

We tried it a few times.

"Okay. Good. You sing quite nicely, and your pronunciation is good. We could continue our English session with some pronouns and verb conjugations. Or we could end our English session and go into American history. What would you rather do?"

Just then, a panel opened, and a small bag dropped to the floor. I got up and discovered a very small bag of Cheetos and a squeezable bag of coconut oil. I gave Mr. Park the Korean note inside the bag, opened the Cheetos bag, and began to eat.

"They're going to give us some dark later on. They will warn us," said Mr. Park.

"Okay. Boy, these are good. Have you ever eaten Cheetos?"

"I don't think so. I don't think I've ever had any."

I stopped as I put the last Cheeto to my mouth, "I guess you'll have to come and get it," putting it halfway in my mouth.

Mr. Park jumped up, "Stop." He grabbed my face, put his mouth to mine, crunched on the Cheeto, opened my lips with his tongue, got the whole thing, and ate it.

Pushing him back and wiping my mouth with the back of my hand, I looked at him for a minute and said, "Well, how was it?"

"Salty... nicely salty."

"Maybe we really do need some lunch," I said.

I put the rice and water in the rice cooker. Mr. Park sliced the tofu and placed it in a small basket at the top of the rice cooker. There were several sides in the refrigerator which we set out on the counter.

As we ate, we discussed our next lessons and decided to start some Korean language lessons. He was going to teach me some K-pop-type dancing later.

Mr. Park started Korean lessons.

"안녕하세요!" (An-nyong ha-se-yo? --Hello?) I repeated it. (I have heard about it often on Korean TV shows.)

"처음 뵙겠습니다?" (Cho-um boep-get-sup-ni-da? --How do you do?) I tried to repeat it. He frowned and said it again. I tried it again. He said it was better.

"내 이름은 박해진입니다. My name is Mr. Park Hae Jin. 이름이 뭐에요? What is your name?"

I tried to repeat this. He frowned and said it again. He tried again. I failed again. He said, "That's the worst pronunciation I have ever heard."

I said, "See, I'm already excelling at being the worst! Worst at hiccups and worst at Korean pronunciation."

He got up quickly and walked away, saying loudly over his shoulder, "It's time for a break."

Much later we started the dancing lesson. I warned him that I was a terrible dancer.

He said to himself, "Is there anything she's not terrible at?" But calmly and seemingly sweetly, he said. "We'll just practice until you get it. It's not like we're booked up for activities. Watch me."

He started to hum and did various steps as he hummed.

"You have a pretty nice voice," I said.

"Thank you. I'll sing along this time, and maybe this will help with your Korean too."

He began to sing and dance at the same time.

"So, what are the lyrics about?"

"They're about a young man longing for a lovely woman. Now, you stand here and do the steps I do."

He sang and danced to the first line. I tried to copy his steps. We tried the first line again and again and again. Occasionally, he would stop, grab me by both arms and sing the first line right to my face-enunciating clearly. I have to admit I began to sing the first line properly, but the dancing was still clearly a disaster.

After about an hour, frustrated with my lack of progress, he said, "I need a break! I don't think I can stand to look at your face for another minute!"

I looked up at the ceiling gods and yelled, "Send down a ski mask, please."

Mr. Park stalked off to the bathroom, which was actually where I wanted to go.

"I hope you're quick in there because I have to go," I said.

"Just wait!" he yelled back.

I began to pace up and down because I really had to go.

Just at that moment, the lights began to flash. I jumped and crouched against the wall since we had been in "daylight" the whole time. Mr. Park came out and said, "This must be the warning before they give us some dark."

I ran into the bathroom, used the toilet, brushed my teeth, and then the lights went out. I felt my way out of the bathroom and fell over onto the mattress on top of Mr. Park. We both screamed.

"Sorry, sorry," I said. "When they say dark they mean dark."

We arranged ourselves in our usual back-to-back sleeping style and managed to pull the blanket over ourselves.

After a while, I said, "Are you asleep?"

He said, "No, I'm still too frustrated at you."

"Could you sing the song to which we were trying to dance to me? I could practice in the dark until we get sleepy."

"Okay," he said and sang the first phrase. I sang it afterward.

"Not bad," he said. He sang the second line, which we really hadn't practiced before. I massacred it. He was quiet for a while.

"Okay," he said. "Let's turn over and face each other - just for this line and I'll sing so that you can hear the sounds better."

We both turned over and reoriented ourselves by feeling with our hands. Finally, he began to sing again. After about three times, I could feel myself falling asleep.

Chapter 5
Having Loud Sex in the Camera-Free Zone

Several hours later, the lights suddenly came on. I was on my back, and he was on his side facing me with one arm and one leg over me. I looked at his sweet face and thought, "I really have to go to the bathroom."

Squirming sideways on the mattress, I was pretty successful at getting out of there until I fell eight inches or so to the floor with a thud. Mr. Park woke up a little and turned over to his usual position facing the opposite way.

I sat up, smiled, and headed to the bathroom. After doing my business and brushing my teeth, I took a shower and got dressed. Miraculously, Mr. Park slept through it all. He must have been really tired after instructing me the day before.

He hopped up, went to the bathroom, and came out ready to do his (or our) daily exercises. I had folded up the blanket and pushed the mattress to the middle of the floor. He proceeded to do pushups and squats while I did my side bends and some jumping jacks. Then, we were off to the races around the room. I did this for 15 times and then plopped down on the mattress. Mr. Park continued on his disciplined way - round and round. I closed my eyes, lay back on the bed, and fell back to sleep. Later, Mr. Park shook me awake, and we had breakfast. I cleaned up the kitchen.

Sitting on the bed to discuss our day, we noticed a black object fluttering down from the ceiling. Mr. Park jumped up and grabbed it. It was a black ski mask. We both smiled. He brought it over to me.

I put it on and said, "So when we can't stand each other's faces, the person who is irritating the hell out of the other one can put this on."

I pulled the mask over my face. It just revealed my eyes and mouth. Mr. Park stared at me for a while. Finally, he said, "Maybe it will work, but you may have to go sit in the corner facing the wall, too."

"Now you try it on, and I'll take a look."

After he put on the ski mask, one glance told me. "Under no circumstances are you putting this on."

"Why?" he asked innocently.

"Let's go look in the mirror."

We rushed into the bathroom. I pushed him over in front of the mirror.

"Maybe you don't realize it, but I have watched you many times in *Man to Man*. Often, I had the thought that you looked like a frog."

He turned to me, "A frog?

"Hear me out! I thought your saving graces were your expressive eyes and your eyebrows. Now, this just emphasizes your frog-like yet oddly beautiful lips. Even though I might be mad at you, wouldn't this just make me want to see you more, not less?" I put my fingers up to his lips in the mirror.

He was right behind me and somehow his arm was around my waist. "Do you see what I mean?" I asked to the mirror. His lips seemed to just jump out of the mask!

Ever the narcissist, he asked, "Do you think my lips need moisturizing? Could you put some of your coconut oil on them?"

I looked down and noticed the squeezable coconut oil was on the cabinet next to the sink.

"Are you serious?" I grabbed the coconut oil, put a little on my fingertip, turned around, and smeared it over his lips a few times. "Is that good enough?"

He glanced into the mirror. "They may need a little blotting," he said as he leaned down and kissed me.

"Back off," I said. "Take that mask off!"

I stalked away to the bedroom and sat down on the mattress. He came in and tossed the mask to me. "The mask was your idea. Who knew a mask could be a sex toy?"

"Come over here and sit down."

He did so eagerly.

"Remain calm. Let's talk quietly so those up above may not be able to hear us."

"Okay," he said.

"The people up above seem to have listening devices, and they probably have cameras. They could see everything we do down here. They could be filming us," I said quietly. "For all we know, they could have us streaming 24 hours a day.

"It would be good to know if there are any 'safe zones' where they can't see us or hear us. I would hope so for the bathroom. Maybe you could ask if they can see us, even in the bathroom?"

"I'll try that," he said. "What else?"

"Now that we have the 'dark', I suppose we could engage in any hanky-panky we want during that time."

"Hanky-panky? I don't know what that means. What is it?" he asked.

"Fooling around?"

"What?"

"Oh, for God's sake! Having sex or sex play, that kind of thing."

"Did you think because I kissed you, I wanted to have sex with you?" His voice had gotten a little bit louder.

"I may have noticed a slight warm spot on my back when you had your arm around my waist."

There seemed to be laughter in the heavens.

"I guess their mics are pretty sensitive," I said.

Mr. Park grabbed the blanket and put it over the top of our heads. "Let's whisper. I don't want to have sex with you. You are old."

"So true," I said. "But surprisingly enough, I wouldn't mind kissing you every once in a while, when you're particularly sweet. Also, I'm pretty good at rubbing things."

We stared at each other in the dimness under the blanket. He laughed, put his arms around me, and we had a nice long kiss. We removed our arms away from the other person and came out from under the blanket. I went to sit over by a wall. He yelled our question about cameras in the bathroom upwards and we sat there thinking.

Finally, I said, "I think it might be fun to go over *Man to Man* since I have watched it so many times."

"You mean the K-drama where you thought I looked like a frog?"

"Yeah, that one."

He frowned. "If I looked like a frog, how come you watched it so many times?"

"I used to wash dishes while watching the show and you looked like a frog a couple of times."

"You washed dishes while watching *Man to Man*! How?"

"I would prop up my cell phone on the windowsill above the sink. Overall, I would say it's a comedy and watching it would cheer me up every day. You were tremendously funny in it just by the use of your eyes and eyebrows."

"Thank you," he said.

"Your lips came into play a few times also."

"Weren't they wonderful?" he asked cheekily.

"Yes...Anyway, I thought the hero of the story was Ungwang and you were the eye candy."

"What?! Why do you say that?"

"Ungwang's character articulated the values of family, loyalty, and love. He verbally defended Dong-Hyun and convinced Guard Kim that killing people wasn't the way to go. He publicly confronted a corrupt CEO. He did everything with his humor and grace still intact. As a civilian, he went off to save Do-ha and lent Guard Kim $5,000,000. He stood by Guard Kim as a brother."

"Okay, I get that, but what about the love story between Guard Kim and Do-ha?"

"Truthfully, it was a little confusing to me. It was on-again, off-again. It was a lie at times. At times, it was real. When was that time? Your character didn't articulate much. You sat there quietly and attentively-which was perfect at times. At points I just longed for one or two words. The Do-ha character was used to articulate things.

"For example, after you rescued Do-ha from Agent S, you were supposed to get her to sign the swearing-her-to-secrecy paper. Do-ha had really been through a harrowing experience. The camera shows the red marks on her wrists. You look at them, look pained, but say nothing. If only you had reached your hand out, touched the marks, and said, 'What you must have gone through' or something like that. I'd also like the two of you to actually be together at the end not just a dot disappearing and Guard Kim's voice."

"That all seems to be criticism of the script, not me. Frog—where are the frog parts? That's what I want to know!" he shouted.

"There were two times it stood out to me. Firstly, when you received word that Dong-Hyun was hit by a truck, your face transforms from super happy to super concerned-mad-sad in ten seconds or less. It was just after maybe the only truly fabulously-happy smile I'd seen in the story up to that point, so I re-watched it a few times. A frog jumped out at me. Let's go look in the mirror, and you can re-enact it."

"Okay," he said, and we both ran into the bathroom.

"You, Guard Kim, have just run over to tell Do-ha that all your assignments are completed, and you are all hers now. (Oddly, she doesn't seem too enthusiastic about it.) You have the most beautiful smile of the whole show, and your eyes are sparkling." Mr. Park re-enacted the scene. "Suddenly, you receive a phone call, quickly transform into a frog, and leave."

Mr. Park re-enacts the scene while looking in the mirror.

"Well?" I asked.

"I get what you're saying, but I can't help how I look unless you want me to get surgery."

"No, never," I said, somewhat flustered. "In fact, now that I think about it, the contrast of your smile and your frown may have cemented for me the beauty of your smiling face, at least as I look back on it."

"You're weird," he said.

"I know. Anyway, I forgot to mention your pathetic face. I loved it so much."

He looked at me disgustedly.

"Your pathetic face is the one when you look up at Do-ha (after purportedly being recently shot in the gut) as she asks if you want to do it again, and you give a little pleading nod. The 'it' in this case appears to be 'have sex'."

"You mean this face?" while looking pathetically sexy at me.

A piece of paper fell from the ceiling. Mr. Park scooped it up, turned to me, and said, "They say the toilet area has no cameras." We looked at each other. Mr. Park raised his index finger, pointing upward. "To the toilet!" he exclaimed.

We rushed into the bathroom and ran over to the toilet.

"Martha, would you like to have a seat here on my lap?" he asked loudly.

"I certainly would."

"Would you like to kiss me?"

"Who wouldn't?" We gave each other a quick kiss.

"Well, how was it?" he asked.

"Excellent," I said.

"We've never actually seen each other's body without clothes. Wouldn't this be a good opportunity?"

We were still speaking loudly.

"You may be disappointed," I said quietly.

Loudly, I said, "Well, the thing is that my boobs can do tricks."

There's a loud crash up above in the ceiling.

I stood up, went across to the sink, grabbed the coconut oil, and headed back to the toilet. "Are you ready for this?" (Loudly.)

Mr. Park gave me his best pathetic look, then smiled devilishly. I took off my shirt and slowly rubbed my boobs with oil. They began to do their tricks.

"Oh my god," he said. "May I touch them?"

Sounds of more scrambling came from up above.

"If you gently rub more oil on them," I said quietly.

"Unbelievable!" he exclaimed loudly.

Since I was standing right in front of him, I dropped my pants and asked him to apply some oil 'down there.' He did so while I grabbed a towel rack to remain stable.

"Let's take your shirt off," I said.

He quickly removed his shirt and threw it out into the bathroom. I said that we should keep some clothes close so we wouldn't have to move into the cameras with nothing on.

"I notice a large bulge in your pants," hiking up the volume again. "Stand up, and let's see if we'll be able to get those pants off."

It was tough to get his pants off, and one of my eyes got hit by his penis. Finally, we tossed his pants out.

I said loudly, "God bless Korea. Wow!" I then smiled and pointed up to the ceiling. "For such a slender fellow that is gigantic! We may run out of oil rubbing this up!"

I moistened it up for a while with my hands and lips. He just couldn't take it anymore, pushed me back against the wall, and, contrary to his previous declaration, decided to have sex with me. He acted as though he had been deprived of sex for quite a while and really put his back into it. I felt his presence drumming deep inside. He staggered back and sat on the toilet while I slid to the floor. He stood up, pulled me on the toilet seat, and said, "Are you okay?"

"Yes."

He strode out (into the camera area), naked for two feet until he reached the shower. I showered afterward. Finally, we both put on our clothes, and I dried my hair. I discovered Mr. Park asleep on the bed. I got in our normal back-to-back configuration, pulled the blanket up, and fell asleep, too.

Chapter 6
Expanding Ideas for Activities

When we woke up, we noticed that a lot of good food and some treats were on the kitchen counter. There were new towels and lots of coconut oil containers in the bathroom.

"What do you think all this means?" I asked Mr. Park.

"It appears that we must have slept heavily for them to be able to do this. It also means they must have liked the show or at least the sound effects."

"I rather liked it myself. Do you want to do your exercises before we eat?"

"Yeah, it's good to maintain some routine."

The bed went in the middle. He did his squats, stretches, jumping jacks, leg lifts, and body contortions too numerous to name. I lagged behind in my usual manner. We ran around the track for quite a time, until I flung myself on the bed and rested until he finished up. We took some quick showers and came back for some great food.

"Since we pleased 'them' so much, let's ask for a lot of chalk - white and colored. We could fill the walls with our lessons and drawings. Let's brainstorm as many topics as possible as it seems as though we're going to be here for a while longer," I said.

Mr. Park called up our chalk request while we did the dishes. Mr. Park liked to wash, and I liked to dry. While putting things away in the kitchen drawers I found a small note pad and a pencil.

"We could use this to individually list things we could do here. Come over here to the bed and we'll take turns putting our ideas down." I drew a line down the middle of the page and created two columns. I put 'MK Ideas' at the top of one column and 'PHJ Ideas' at the top of the other. It turned out that he wrote in Korean, and I wrote in English.

"Let's write down three ideas on my side and then three ideas on your side. Then we can ask some clarifying questions but try not to get too bogged down until we write as many ideas as we can even if they sound crazy."

"How could anything we come up with be any crazier than the situation we find ourselves in?" he asked,

After translating for me, he had written 'better food', 'more clothing', and 'thorough apartment cleaning'. I took the pad and wrote 'exercises', 'dancing', and 'talking about K-dramas'.

"Your ideas seem like stuff we have already been doing," he said.

"I wanted to make sure they got on the list. Your list seems reasonable, although some of the things are things that our captors would do. Maybe a nice cleaning day would be helpful. Okay, let's each try to brainstorm three more activities."

Martha wrote 'design an apartment or house together', 'draw pictures of each other', and 'talk about fashion'. Hae Jin wrote 'get a night light in the bathroom during the dark-time', 'ask when they will release us', and 'ask what it will take to get them to release us'.

"Once again, your list seems to be about what others can do, not us. Unless you consider the 'asking' as something to do. Maybe we should strategize what and for what purpose we're asking these people for stuff or information. Anyway, you and I could certainly use a discussion about our situation periodically."

"I liked your ideas, they seemed doable," said Mr. Park.

On the next round, Martha wrote 'a map of the world, Korea, and the United States', 'talk about places we visited or lived', and 'talk about friends and hobbies.' Mr. Park wrote 'continue teaching Korean to Martha', 'write a script together', and 'talk about dark-time activities.'

"I think I may need some clarification on that last point," said Martha.

"Gladly. Let's wait until the dark-time comes and I'll do a lot of clarifying," Mr. Park joked. He continued, "These seem to be plenty of ideas for activities for us to do. But I do sense we need to actually have some discussion right now about our situation, questions, and concerns we have, just to try to allay some of our fears or at least get them out so we can come up with a plan or at least have a common understanding of what our stance will be."

"I must admit that I also wrote down many questions about our captors and our potential fate. Some of these were what our relationship would be if we ever got out of here, how can we escape, who is doing this to us, what is their motive, are they really going to let us go or will they kill us?" Martha said.

"I really want to talk or communicate with my family and my agency," said Mr. Park.

"I'm still wondering what those guys up above are thinking. Why, other than our adventure yesterday, are they being nice to us?" asked Martha.

"Me too. I'm not sure if their interest in us is purely personal to them basically, they are bored and want some entertainment - or if this is some big plot by someone who tells them what to do."

"I'm willing to entertain them, to a certain extent, if we can get some concessions in our living conditions or our release," Martha said. "But I'm not sure how far I'm willing to go. If it will save our lives or get us out of here, I may go further than I ever believed I could."

"Calm yourself. Whatever you're thinking may not come up," said Mr. Park. "Let's start with all our requests and see what happens next." He spoke to the ceiling about chalk, more protein, some more clothes, and a nightlight for the bathroom. "Finally, we want to know when or under what circumstances you will release us. On a personal note, I want to talk to my agency and my family. Please reply to all these requests."

"Do you want to discuss any other of the items on our lists?" I asked.

"Yes, I'm curious about us designing a house or apartment together and our future relationship. What did you mean by listing those things?"

"Now that I look at those items on my list, I'm wondering what I was thinking. I know, under brainstorming protocols, people are supposed to be free to say whatever they feel or whatever they're thinking that's relevant to the topic. Maybe those items just popped out of my subconscious? I have always had an interest in interior design and furnishings, so I thought it would just be a fun thing to do. If we pretend it's for us - you and me - I thought, it would be a fun activity."

"I kind of like interior design too, so maybe it would be fun. I'm okay with that," said Mr. Park.

"As for any future relationship," I said, "after this is over - whenever that is - I think our relationship is changing every minute and every day here. Right now, it seems to me, that if they let us out today, I might be able to say, 'nice meeting you' and get on a plane and go to Malaysia. But every activity and every conversation is rapidly expanding our knowledge of each other. I can foresee that after another week, I would want to make sure you're adjusting back to your family and your career. After an additional week, I may not be able to let go of your hand or not be able to go a day without seeing you."

Mr. Park looked down at the floor. He said, "Maybe I'll be better able to cope with this because I'm often acting in some cast for several months at a time. I'm used to 'pretend relationships' that don't go anywhere."

"So, have you been using your pretending skills?" I asked.

"Yes, to some extent."

"I guess I could pretend, but at my age, it doesn't seem worth the effort," I said. I was disappointed in his answer.

"The only difference is that we're not acting, at least I think we're actually, truly in this situation. But even if we're here for a long time, there are so many things that separate us, particularly our age difference. How could we overcome that and have any kind of future relationship, other than just being friends?" he asked.

"It does seem far-fetched, doesn't it? ... I guess we'll just have to ponder this as time passes," I said. "Let's take a break and practice our dance."

And so began a long period of a normalized routine, punctuated by a few trips "to the toilet" when we thought we needed something special from the guys up above. The "lofty powers" gave us better food, clothing, and a nightlight for the bathroom during dark-time. But Hae Jin (as I now called him) and I began a regular sex time when the dark came. We tried many positions under the cover of the real darkness of a closed-up room. A lot of laughing was involved. Almost all the positions were great. A few were complete duds - either I didn't feel like doing it, he didn't feel like doing it, or we were just exhausted.

Chapter 7
Sex Show for the Ceiling Gods

However, I noticed and so did Mr. Park that our nighttime closeness leaked over into our daytime activities. We somehow ended up holding hands during language lessons. Once we were so happy agreeing about some K-drama that we actually kissed while laughing about it. Several times while doing exercises we collided and ended up having mini-wrestling matches on the mattress. Sometimes we'd just sit in a corner of the room, put our arms around each other, and take a nap.

After one such nap, we woke up and Mr. Park kissed me sweetly.

I said, "You do know they're watching us?"

"I don't care anymore what they think," he said.

Naturally, all kinds of noises broke out above.

"I agree that they are watching us, Ms. Karr," said Mr. Park. "Let's give them a little show. Spread out your legs here on the floor and I'll sit in between them with my legs draped over your thighs and our crotches touching."

"Are you sure this is going to end up just a 'little show'?" I asked.

"I'm not sure of anything these days," he said as he sat between my thighs. "Scoot closer to me and give me a kiss." Instead of waiting for me to scoot closer, he grabbed my butt, pushed me to his crotch, and kissed me quite dangerously and extensively.

Getting into the spirit of the 'show', I said, "Now, I'll lean back in an arch, and you can put your hands on my breasts."

"Certainly," he said. "But after that, we're going to have to head to the 'toilet'."

I looked at him quizzically as I slowly leaned back, and he put his hands on my boobs. "The girls are acting up," I said.

I jumped up and headed to our un-cameraed meeting place. He stood up a little more gingerly and made his way to the bathroom. I had already removed my clothes. We wrestled off his pants and proceeded to party while making incredibly loud noises for the crowd overhead. He then just walked out boldly, took a shower, dried off, and got dressed. I headed out a little later and did the same things while attempting to keep my breasts hidden by my hands. Afterward, I went out into the bedroom.

"Okay, this is a problem," I said.

"What's the problem?" he asked.

"You are the problem. How can I have sex all night and now I have to have sex all day, too?"

The upstairs broke into applause!

"Come to think of it - are you guys putting Viagra or some other penis-enhancing product into our food, water, or air?" I shouted up to the ceiling.

Hae Jin looked hurt. A piece of paper fluttered down from the ceiling. Mr. Park grabbed it. "It says they are absolutely not 'enhancing me'."

"Let me see that," I said.

The note was in Korean but by now I'm pretty good at reading Korean and can confirm that's what the note said. Mr. Park suddenly looked amazingly proud of himself.

"I hope you're not about to prance around the room in some sort of cave-man bragging rite," I said.

"Not a bad idea," he said as he proceeded to go round the mattress with his arms outstretched and a big smile on his face.

"I don't know why you're so proud of yourself! During your measly 4 or 5 orgasms last night I probably had 15 and I had another couple just now in the bathroom!"

I hopped up and paraded around the room with my arms outstretched like some conquering hero.

More applause from up above.

I stared at the ceiling. "These guys are better than God or 'the gods' - they actually give you feedback."

Mr. Park looked up, "You're right."

We stared at each other - our arms still outstretched to the sides. I shook my chest provocatively. He moved one of his eyebrows - provocatively. We walked around the mattress and met for a big hug.

He whispered in my ear, "Weren't you exaggerating a little bit about orgasm numbers? It doesn't seem like you're really that mad at me."

"I am really mad at you," I said. I leaned back and looked at his beautiful face. "But it's hard to stay mad... Were you born under the 'beautiful star'?" I asked.

"Of course, as were you," he answered.

"You're sweet, but a liar," I responded.

He leaned down and kissed me for a while.

I broke away and spent some time trying to breathe properly. "It seems like we need to get back to our lessons or come up with some calming down activities," I said. "What about asking for a puzzle for us to do? It could also make a nice 'getaway' activity for one person to work on by themselves."

Mr. Park immediately called up for a couple of puzzles. "Today, why don't we work on the apartment idea that you thought of a week or two ago?" he asked.

"Okay!" I jumped up, grabbed a piece of chalk, and started asking questions. "What country do you think this apartment should be in?" I asked.

"Well, I like the idea of Malaysia, but Bali, Vietnam, and Thailand would be good, too."

I wrote down all these ideas. "Maybe let's just start with Malaysia and later we can develop other ideas for the other countries. How many bedrooms should the apartment have?"

"I was thinking three to four, especially if my family comes to visit," said Hae Jin.

"Four sounds good." I went to the wall and drew a vertical line with some of our new chalk. "You draw your apartment here and I'll draw my proposed apartment over there."

"Maybe we should include furniture, too," said Mr. Park.

I began to draw a blueprint for myself. It had an entry into basically a wide hall with a living room, kitchen, dining room, and a balcony on the beach side. On either side of this main living area, there were two bedrooms and two baths. I figured they could be adapted for different uses. On one side there was a master bedroom with its own balcony and a large bath/closet on the inside wall. That made the wall on the other side of the bathroom much smaller, so I made it an office with its own small bath. On the other side, I had two equal-sized bedrooms with two baths - one for each bedroom between them. I figured out all the closet space and door openings. Then I "painted" each room by using colored chalk (loosely based on the Pa Qua principles of color) and drew in some little furniture ideas - beds, couches, chairs, exercise equipment, and kitchen equipment.

Mr. Park had a totally different approach with a hall entry with a small office to the right. The hall came into the living room with a smaller hallway to the left that led to the three bedrooms. The master bedroom faced the beach, as in my design. However, the kitchen and dining room ran parallel to the wall of the master bedroom and offered a breakfast or reading nook before the balcony.

Once we were finished, we looked at the other person's ideas and began to make comments.

"Your design looks pretty utilitarian," said Mr. Park.

"You're right. I think I need a blocking wall between the entry and the living room to confuse wayward forces that may try to come in, as accords with feng shui."

"Do you know feng shui?" asked Hae Jin.

"Only vaguely. I read some books on it many years ago. Do you?"

"Not really. I'm sort of like you. I skimmed a few books long ago," he said.

"I like your design a lot. It seems much more 'homey', by that I mean more welcoming and livable. What colors do you like?"

"Maybe I'm influenced by current trends which give a more 'masculine' and luxurious look to a room through dark colors like a dark olive green or a deep blue with Afghan rugs and strategically spaced lamps. I'm not sure if this would be appropriate for an apartment on the beach though."

"In my house in the U.S., I used the Pa Qua system generally to determine my room colors. My living room had cream-colored walls with turquoise trim and light blue window shades. The east-facing bedroom was a beautiful mint green, and the southern bedroom was butter colored. My den was tourmaline with a white ceiling that I hand-plastered. My kitchen was a lobster bisque. I also had a small alcove near the laundry room where I did most of my writing. The walls were clay colored with an accent wall of dark blue. After my whole house was painted the way I wanted it to be painted, I felt strangely happy and at peace. It's amazing how calming everything is when it's exactly the way you want it."

We were both seated together again, both in lotus positions in front of the wall, holding hands.

"Navajos, a Native American tribe has some similar concepts about associating colors with the seasons and the four directions. Some of these colors are about the color of the sky or how the light looks in certain seasons. So yellow is associated with summer and white with winter. Things look different in different lighting."

"Of course, in the film industry lighting is key," said Hae Jin.

"You know, I was thinking that maybe we should eliminate the offices here and just have a large bathroom/dressing room in case we're bringing in sand from the beach."

"Do you think we'll be at the beach a lot?" he asked.

"Maybe at beach bars or maybe swimming pools. I can't tolerate much sunshine because of my fair skin, but maybe we could design a full-body swimsuit."

"We could just put you in a large trash bag at that rate," he joked. "What do you foresee us doing then?"

"I'd like to go on long walks in the cool of the morning, come home, cook some breakfast, clean up, go shopping or to art galleries or museums, take a nap, get food at one of the night markets, sit on our balcony and watch the ships go by. What about you?'

"Well, I think I'd have to keep working for as long as possible, so maybe this apartment would have to be someplace in Korea. I'd like to have a nice big bed with clean sheets every night. A padded headboard would allow us to sit up, read or hold hands, put our arms around each other, kiss, make love, and rest.

"Your ideas seem pretty specific," I said.

"Thank you."

"Let's go eat lunch!"

Chapter 8
Puzzles Arrive-A Fight Ensues

After lunch and dishes, we decided to work on U.S. state capitals. So, we drew a giant map on the wall as best we could and tried to figure out what the states were and what the capitals were. To get to fifty states was quite a struggle and then we argued over the capitals. Mr. Park seemed to know them as much as I did. Occasionally, I would throw in a history lesson about a particular state. We drew in some rivers, mountains, and lakes. It was quite a masterpiece by the time it was done.

We had a lot of chalk all over our clothes, our hair, faces, and hands. We shook out our clothes in the shower, took quick showers, and ate dinner. The dark seemed to come early that night, and we went to sleep quickly in each other's arms.

Hae Jin was getting a bit frisky in the early morning dark-time when the lights suddenly came on. He paused for a second and a package fell from the ceiling to the floor. During that pause, I threw the blanket over his backside, and he proceeded to finish his project. We were breathing pretty heavily.

"What the fuck!" yelled Hae Jin to the ceiling.

The sound of applause came from above and a voice actually spoke. "It's as we suspected. We are suspending the dark hours for now," it said.

"Why?" I asked. "Do you want us to fuck or not, because it seems like you've been cheering us on."

"We're thinking about it. Goodbye," the voice from the ceiling answered.

"Well, we got caught that time and the cameras were rolling," I said to Hae Jin. "Do you think they'll sell the video?"

"How the hell should I know?" He looked very angry.

"If they sell it, won't that spark a massive search for you? Wouldn't it not be to their advantage?" I asked.

"If there hasn't been a search for me by now, why would you think there would be one after seeing my backside?"

"I would definitely search for you after seeing your backside."

He laughed and said, "But that's just you."

I lowered my voice, "Speaking of which, as you well know, I was left in the lurch back there with some unfinished business. Could you help me out a bit either here or in the toilet?"

Hae Jin stood up and said, "To the toilet!"

We traveled to the toilet area with the blanket wrapped around us. He closed the toilet lid and sat down. I sat on his lap and arched my back while my tricky boobs called out for relief and my vagina got relief via his fingers. By this time, being a healthy boy, he had sprung up again and I was forced(?) to be polite and sit on that healthy equipment and we both came together. We hit the shower, got dressed, and came out to the bedroom.

"What's in the package they sent down before when we were so rudely interrupted?" I asked.

He opened the package and said, "It's a couple of puzzle boxes."

"I hope they're not X-rated!"

Fortunately, there were a couple of pastoral scenes - one with a cabin on a lake and one with a waterfall and a fisherman downstream.

"Maybe we should try one of these just to calm us down a little and get our minds off recent events."

We poured out the puzzle on the floor in a corner of the room and began to turn all the pieces over.

"What do you like to do first?" I asked.

"Doesn't everyone want to do the outside edge pieces first?"

"I'll help you find edge pieces, but I like to work in the center and then hook up with the frame later."

"Why?"

"I'm attracted to the colors and how they go together. I like to find little scenes or little areas and piece those together. Then I can start placing them in the frame and find attaching pieces."

"It sounds like you've done a lot of puzzles," Mr. Park said.

"When you're seventy-five and have been married for 50 years - most of those pre-internet - you've done a lot of puzzles."

"I still can't believe you're 75."

"Me either," I said, "but isn't this white hair a clue?" I pointed to the part in my hair which was white as my hair kept growing out, revealing the true hair color.

"I suppose."

We began our respective tasks - he on the frame and I on the center. I sat for a while and began to arrange the pieces by colors and by any man-made construction that stood out in the pieces. We each would ask for the box with the picture on it until we finally got into a fight about who needed it the most. Then we had a little wrestling match over the box and basically messed up all the work we had done.

"Look at the mess you've made," I yelled.

"Me? What about you!" he yelled back.

For some reason, I don't know why, I burst into tears. Then, for some reason, he burst into tears. We put our arms around each other and cried.

"Are you getting snot all over my shirt, Mr. Park?"

"I am, Ms. Karr," and he proceeded to wipe his eyes and nose on my shirt.

"Let's go wash our faces in the bathroom and get new shirts on," I said.

We held hands as we walked to the sink and removed our shirts. (I had a bra on.) I washed his face with a face cloth, and he washed mine.

"I don't want you to be sad, Mr. Park."

"I wasn't sad until you were sad. Why did you cry?"

"That was the first time you yelled at me since the first day we came here. You yelled quite a lot that day."

"But you yelled at me first!" he said.

"Did I?... I'm so sorry."

We found new shirts, put them on, and began to re-organize the puzzle pieces again.

"I think we're a little stressed out. Maybe we've become attached to each other in some unhealthy ways," I said.

"Because we yelled at each other and cried? That doesn't seem unhealthy in our circumstances."

"Maybe it is healthy in here, but if we ever get back to the outside world, it won't be," I said.

"Who says we're going to get back?" asked Mr. Park.

I nodded in agreement.

Chapter 9
Hae Jin's Hair Turns White

We made it a point to "play nicely" on the puzzle after that day. I helped with the edges first with Mr. Park. Then Hae Jin helped me with the "innards". Three days later, which included other activities like running, dancing, math, and Korean, the puzzle was finished except for one piece which was missing.

We decided to do a 'run' around the room, put the mattress in the middle, and started jogging. The puzzle was in a corner of the room and out of the running path. We had a new game where I would actually chase him because I was so much faster and fitter than I was in the beginning. If I launched myself properly, I could sometimes tackle him as he passed me, and we would end up in a wrestling match on the bed.

On this day, however, while rounding a corner, I slipped on something (which turned out to be the lost puzzle piece) and everything went black for me. When I woke up, I was in a hospital room, hooked up to an IV. A doctor with a mask on came in and said I had had a concussion and a contusion that bled a lot. Standing next to the doctor was a man with a mask on but without a doctor's coat on. In order to get to the cut on my head they said they had shaved my head and not to be alarmed by that. I had several stitches. The doctor said my stitches would gradually dissolve, but I'd have to use a shower cap to keep my head dry for a week or two. The doctor left the room, but the other man stayed.

I said, "Where is Mr. Park?"

"He is where you last saw him."

"Is there something wrong with him?" I asked because his tone of voice seemed strained to me.

"We were thinking of letting you go in some distant city, but it appears we need you for a while longer."

"What's wrong with him?"

"You'll see when you meet him. We're bringing some knitted caps for you and some socks with rubber soles, so you guys won't slip when you run around. I hope you'll be willing to help him."

"Of course, I'll help him if I can. Have you hurt him?"

"No, we haven't. I'm going to sedate you, and you will wake up beside him. Please remain calm when you see him. Can you do that?"

"Yes."

With that, he shot something into the IV port.

I woke up later at what had become my home. I had a knitted cap on my head. Mr. Park was lying beside me. His hands and feet were tied together with long strips of cloth, and his hair had turned completely white. His hands and face had bruises on them. I just sat there, put my hand over his, and waited. Soon he woke up and wildly looked around.

"Calm down, Jin. I'm here with you and I'm all right. I'm going to untie you soon. But first I want to tell you something." I brushed his hair back from his face, smiled, and kissed him.

"Something has happened to you maybe you already know about it. Maybe you've also hurt yourself in other ways. We'll find out when I untie you. Anyway, the thing that has happened to you has happened to many people who have suffered a shock. It happened to one of my brothers. I don't think it will affect your career as an actor, so you don't have to worry about that." I paused for a moment. "Your hair has turned completely white."

"I don't care about that. What about you? Are you okay?"

"Yes, I'm fine. I had a big cut on my head and bled for a while and got knocked out. But I've had a change too. They shaved my head!"

"You're kidding. So, I have white hair and you're bald!"

We both started laughing. I untied him as quickly as possible, and we hurried to the bathroom mirror. I took off my knitted cap.

"Oh, my God!" I screamed.

He looked at me and fake-screamed, "Oh, my God!"

I hit him on the arm. He flinched.

"What's wrong with your arm? Did they beat you up?" I demanded. "Take off your shirt."

He did so and his arms and hands were covered in bruises and wounds.

He explained, "After you fell, some men came down from the ceiling. They had masks on. I fought them for a while, but they quickly gave me an injection, and that knocked me out.

When I woke up, I started hitting the walls with my shoulders. I yelled, "Where's Martha? Is she alive? What have you done with her? Bring her back! I even began to bang my head on the wall. The men reappeared, gave me another shot, and I woke up with you by my side."

I think from all the injections we've been getting we need to drink a bunch of water and eat something. First, let's look at your hair."

His hair was a tangled mess which I worked on for about half an hour until it lay down his back in a brilliant snowfall. His hair was long since it hadn't been cut during the time we had been here. We looked in the mirror, and he looked like a Joseon prince with his beautiful hair and beard. His eyebrows were still black.

"You're still beautiful! Go take a nice soapy shower and then we'll bandage everything that needs bandaging. I'll see if we've got anything to eat."

There was some warm porridge sitting on the kitchen counter with a nearby box of Band-Aids and bandages and a tube of an antibiotic cream. As Hae Jin stepped out of the shower and toweled off, I put ointment and Band-Aids on the bad spots. Mostly, he just seemed bruised. He combed out his hair, got dressed, put on our new skid-reducing socks, and sat down to eat. There were a couple of bottles of orange juice on the counter which we decided to trust and proceeded to sit on the floor and eat.

"This porridge has some sort of sea creature in it I think," I said to Hae Jin. "What is it?"

"It looks and tastes like abalone."

"I have allergies to some seafood," I said.

"Be careful then. Eat a bite and wait a couple of minutes to see if there is a reaction."

I took a bite (it was delicious) and waited.

"Are you sure you're okay with having white hair?" I asked.

"No, I'm not sure. It is quite shocking to look at myself. I know I can dye it any color if I need to though - if I still have a career left."

Lowering my voice as much as possible, I said, "Your white hair and whatever craziness you experienced or performed, convinced them to bring me back to you. One of the 'gods' said they were planning to drop me off in some other city here in Korea."

"Did you see one of them?"

"Yes, but he had a mask on."

"Did he say anything else?"

"Not really - just asked if I was willing to go back and I said yes of course."

Hae Jin smiled. "Why? You could have escaped."

"How did I know that? He might have just killed me."

Hae Jin 's smile went away. "So, you're saying you didn't come back because of me, but to save yourself?" He looked at me so earnestly that my heart nearly broke.

"In a way, yes, but it was not my first or primary reason. Right now, we both need to stay alive for each other. I need to be here to protect you. You need to be here to protect me.

"I'm not having a reaction to the abalone, so let's eat lunch."

After lunch and dishes, we sat in a corner so we could talk some more.

"Are you upset with me because I didn't say I came back because of you?" I asked.

"Yes, I guess I am!" he said defiantly.

"I know we're feeling things right now that we probably shouldn't be feeling. But as far as I can tell I'm in love with you, Hae Jin, and I'd like to tell the four corners of the universe or at least our universe. Stand up, please. We've got our new socks on. We're going on a journey." I took his hand.

I looked up at the ceiling. "First corner of the universe, I love Mr. Park."

He looked a little startled, "What will the ceiling guys think?"

"Who cares?" I yelled. I dragged him to the second corner. "Second corner, I love Hae Jin."

We ran together to the third corner. "Third corner of the universe, I love Jin."

He picked me up and carried me to the fourth corner. "To clarify, old great Fourth Corner, I love Mr. Park Hae Jin."

He put me down and we kissed.

"Well, now that you mention it, I guess I love you, Ms. Karr."

"You guess!"

He gave me another (better) kiss.

"I guess you do. I'm glad you took such a measured approach to our 'true love'!"

He suddenly yelled up to the ceiling, "I love Ms. Martha Karr," and proceeded to give me an even better kiss. The ceiling applauded.

"Could we request a couple of hours of darkness?" he yelled as we fell on the bed. The lights went off. We took our clothes off and made love for a long time. We were fast asleep when the lights came back on.

Chapter 10
The Buddha and Santa Claus Sitting under a Tree

After showering and putting on clean clothes, we ate some sandwiches which the ceiling gods dropped down. We then adjourned to a nearby wall.

"I've been thinking it would be fun to draw some portraits of each other," I said.

"I'm not much of an artist," said Mr. Park.

"Me either, but it seems like we'll have plenty of time to perfect them. I think your hair is too fly-away and not good for running around the room for exercise. I'd like to braid it, but I don't know how to braid plus I think I'd need some rubber bands or scrunchies to do it."

"Let's ask the ceiling. Could you guys send down a braiding booklet and scrunchies for us?" he asked.

"Why don't you sit over there in a lotus position, and I'll draw you as a Buddha sitting under a large tree," I said.

I began to draw him, while he remained surprisingly still. His white hair and beard tumbled down his shirt so that he looked like an old Jesus. I supposed that if I had just drawn him a few days ago, he would have looked like a young Jesus. I was overcome momentarily by what had happened to him. He seemed to be lost in thought or maybe he was just lost and didn't seem to notice my distress. I asked him why he was so still.

"I'm used to this - maintaining my position if I need to. Also, when you mentioned braiding my hair, I could suddenly imagine a scene on a K-drama that had you braiding my hair 50 different ways in a matter of two minutes or so to indicate us having a lot of fun and to indicate a long passage of time."

"You're so clever. Look at my preliminary sketch and tell me what you think."

He twisted up his lips as he studied the drawing, "It looks very preliminary, I would say because I'm much better looking than that!"

"It's time for me to draw you so you're going to have to take off your cap," he said.

"Why? I'll look horrible!"

"And I don't!? If I had a red sweater, I'd look like Santa Claus!"

"Okay, okay," I said. I sat against the wall in a lotus position.

"You look like the real Buddha, and your head should be easy to draw since I could just draw it as a bowling ball." Which he proceeded to do.

"When you least expect it, Buddha will choke you," I said, and I smiled my most Nirvana-like smile.

"I'll look forward to it," as he proceeded to work on his drawing of me and the tree, too.

After he was done, I jumped up to see the result. His drawing was much better than mine.

"I like the tree," I said.

"We'll just name this *The Buddha and Santa Claus Sitting Under a Tree.*" He picked up some red chalk and drew in a red sweater for Santa.

A few days later a bundle fell from the ceiling with a nice red sweater, a braiding booklet, and some scrunchies and rubber bands.

When Mr. Park put on the red sweater and said, "Ho, ho, ho," he did look a lot like Santa.

I began to examine the sweater, "This is a very nice sweater. I see that it's made in Ireland. And it's pretty long. This could be a very convenient item."

"Maybe you could examine it more thoroughly if I were lying on the bed." He flopped over onto the mattress.

"So true." I knelt near him and began to 'notice' the different parts of the sweater by touching each part with my fingers. "I wish I knew more about the knitting patterns used here. The neck, wrists, and bottom hem have a straight-line look, whereas the torso has a twisted cable design. All very beautiful, as is the man wearing it."

"Maybe if you pressed on the patterns a bit more, I too might appreciate the beauty of this sweater."

"You mean here? On your arm?" while touching his arm.

"No, that's not what I meant."

"How about here on your chest?" as I pressed on his chest.

"That's a bit better, I have to admit," he said.

"How about here on your stomach?" where I pressed really hard.

He crinkled over and said, "Ouf. Not quite that hard!"

"What about a little lower on your torso? This sweater is covering up key components if I'm calculating correctly." I moved my hand around that area. "Also, there's a kind of bump down here." My hand kept traveling down to the bump until it seemed to hit the jackpot!

"Be careful!" said a suddenly anxious Mr. Park.

"Something's going on down here," I said. "Maybe your pants are creating some sort of hindrance I'll just remove them for you."

I jumped up, untied the drawstring to his sweatpants, pulled them plus his underpants down his legs, and tossed them behind me. The sweater neatly covered everything.

"Wow, what a sweater!" I said.

I bent over, spread his legs out, and began climbing on my hands and knees between his legs. I lifted the sweater to peek under it. I touched something with my fingers under there. Finally, I decided just to put my head under the sweater, so I could better examine the situation.

From the ceiling, there arose such a clatter and someone yelled, "On Donner, on Blitzen!"

"I guess they think you look like Santa, too."

I was able to continue my examination under the sweater until Mr. Park seemed well satisfied with the result. I did have to hold him down a little bit because, at certain moments, his body was writhing and roiling wildly.

After a shower and rest for Hae Jin and a face wash for me, we looked at the braiding book. Some of the braids were outright complicated.

"Let's just try a simple three-strand braid in the back," I said. I worked on it for a while, and it looked good. Hae Jin liked it too.

"When I was a kid, I saw my Irish grandmother braid her hair. One way was to do it just the way I just did it for you but to the side. Her hair was very long and when she woke in the morning, she just brushed it, pulled it to one side, and softly braided it by herself. Her hair wasn't white like yours, but steel gray. She had braided her hair for over 80 years, so she knew what she was doing. In other words, you could do it for yourself."

"I'll try practicing that," said Hae Jin.

"The other way she braided was to part her hair down the middle and part the hair on the left and right sides. Then she would make a tight braid on both sides and tie them with rubber bands. This would make pigtails on both sides which she would pull up and pin on top of her head, so her hair stayed out of her face all day while she was working. She had 14 children, six of whom had died, so she knew a lot about work."

"She sounds very practical," said Hae Jin.

"She was tough for sure," I said. "I, on the other hand, could only put my hair up in a half-ponytail."

"What's that?"

So, I took out his braid and brushed his hair out again. I sat in front of him and gave him the brush. "So, I'll give you the instructions and you do it yourself. In the future, you can just do it in front of the mirror.

"Brush your hair straight back until it lays down nicely. I'm sorry I don't have any hair of my own to show this. It's easy. Put down your brush. Put a rubber band around the four fingers and thumb of your right hand and stretch your fingers out just enough to hold the rubber band taut. Put your thumbs under your hair on both sides of your face but on top of your ears. Push your thumbs back to the back of your head while accumulating the hair from the sides on your hands. Consolidate the two clumps of hair with the help of your right hand holding the resulting larger clump of hair while the left-hand pulls the rubber band around it. The left hand then twists the rubber band creating an opening, the right hand stuffs the hair through the opening. Let's start now, follow my gestures to help you. Pull your arms up like when a cop says, 'Hands up'." I demonstrated.

He smiled. "Just keep them up, ma'am." He moved forward with dazzling speed placing his face between my breasts and his arms behind my back.

"Sir, do you really want to learn how to do a half-ponytail or not?"

"Not."

"Then, lift up your beautiful face and give me a kiss." Fortunately, we had plenty of free time and were off to the 'races' again.

Later, much later, we began a huge chalk drawing on the wall opposite our map of the United States. It was a map of the world. We decided to put North, Central, and South America to the left; Europe, Africa, the Middle East, and India in the middle; and China, Southeast Asia, Korea, Japan, the Philippines, Australia, and New Zealand to the right. It contained lots of straight lines to indicate coastlines and the general shape of the continents.

This map proved to be a many-day project. Lots of chalk was used and there were many discussions trying to figure out what countries might be where and what the capitals were. Hae Jin was well acquainted with East Asia, so that came in handy. We used different colored chalk for the different major areas. In a way, it was a beautiful and colorful piece of art. Discussions about the history of different areas went along with the map drawing. We told each other about the countries that we had been fortunate to visit or live in. I told him about my husband and my time in the Philippines, Indonesia, Malaysia, Ukraine, Germany, Bosnia, Croatia, and especially Kenya. He told me about China and his experiences in the Philippines and other Southeast Asian nations.

Finally, our minds were just burned out and we had a couple of days napping, singing, dancing, and eating to counteract our mental and artistic efforts. We would go sit under the tree Hae Jin had drawn and attempt to meditate as the Buddha and Santa. At times, it felt as though we were really there in the shade and with a breeze on our faces.

Chapter 11
PHJ Meets Charismatic Adopted Maasai Tribal Member

This phenomenon of being able to transport ourselves to another seemingly real location began to dominate our thinking. I had imagined some things that might happen if ever we were released and told Mr. Park the story I had created in my mind. The story utilized the fact that in Kenya, I had been adopted by the Maasai people. I began to tell the story like this:

Paranae, an adopted member of the Maasai, was invited to talk about how important the Maasai people are to the survival of the planet Earth in the midst of climate change. This short talk was to take place at a TV and movie awards show in Korea. She gave her two-minute speech and was headed backstage where she bumped into Mr. Park Hae Jin who was soon to be introduced on stage to receive an award.

Paranae looked up at Mr. Park and said, "It's the frog," which caused Mr. Park to stop and look at the woman.

Paranae had been invited by Netflix to speak at this awards show. She was working on a project with them that would involve Mr. Park eventually. She had written a novella in which Mr. Park was the main character. Mr. Park had read the novella and was contemplating whether to become involved in the project. The audience and host of the awards show did not know about these impending negotiations.

A cameraman was backstage with a commentator who was supposed to get comments from the award winners after they received their awards.

The cameraman noticed Mr. Park talking to Paranae and pointed his camera and the mic in their direction.

Paranae then said, "Let me take a look at your lips."

Mr. Park bent down slightly.

"No, you're going to have to kneel for me to get a good look."

Mr. Park knelt in front of her.

"Hmmm. May I touch them to see if they are fake?"

"Fake?" Mr. Park smiled. "Sure, give it a try."

She stepped forward a bit and gently ran her index finger over his lips.

"What about a lip-to-lip test?" she asked, as she bent down and kissed him lightly.

Mr. Park stood up abruptly, put his arms around her, and gave her a passionate kiss.

Afterward, Paranae stepped back, bowed, and said, "Nice to meet you," turned, and walked away.

Mr. Park was then called by the host to come on stage to receive his award. After receiving his award, the host said, "By the way, Mr. Park, the crew tells me there were some intriguing moments backstage before you came out. I have no idea what they're talking about, but they want to show this clip taken backstage by our cameraman. Let's take a look."

The video clip, which started from the time Mr. Park knelt before Ms. Paranae, was shown on a large screen on stage. The audience gasped, applauded, then gasped again.

The host said, "I've been told that Paranae has been brought back to the stage to be with us, too. Ms. Paranae can you explain the clip we just saw?"

"I'm not sure I need to. As you can see, he must be an ardent supporter of efforts to address climate change, so he was kneeling before me, I'm sure, out of respect for my minor contribution through my speech today."

The host said, "What about fake lips and kissing?"

"I guess I've always wondered about Korean TV and movie stars' lips - wondering if they're fake - the question just popped into my head. Mr. Park, being polite, merely let me touch them and lightly kiss them to prove the integrity of Korean stars." The audience laughed and applauded loudly.

The host then asked, "Then why did Mr. Park give you such a big hug and kiss?"

"Again, one can only just wonder at the welcoming spirit of Korean men for a foreigner who just arrived in your country yesterday. I must admire them and thank them." The entire audience seemed stunned, then laughed and applauded.

"After that big hug and kiss," said the host, "how could you just walk away and say, 'nice to meet you'?"

"It was nice!" Laughter and applause. "And Mr. Park was being called to the stage."

Frustrated, the host said, "Are you saying this is the first time you've ever met Mr. Park Hae Jin?"

"Yes."

The host turned to PHJ, "What do you have to say about this?"

"I think Ms. Paranae has explained it adequately. Again, I'd like to thank everyone. Ms. Paranae would you like a ride to your hotel?"

She said, "Yes, thank you." To the audience, "Goodbye, everyone!" Applause.

Mr. Park had a car and driver waiting outside the theater's stage door. They quickly hustled into the back seat of the car and were off.

Paranae said, "Would you like to watch the news with me? I'm sure our performance back there will cause quite a stir in the entertainment news."

Park Hae Jin said, "I don't think we can go to your hotel, or it will cause even more of an uproar. We can't go to my house for the same reason. We need to stay out of sight for a few hours."

"Let's ask your driver if we can go to his house," said Paranae. "What's his name and does he speak English?"

"His name is Mr. Kim, but I'll do the asking." Mr. Park talked to the driver for a while. "Surprisingly, he agreed with your suggestion. I've never been to his house, but I know he has a wife and children. This will be a good time to meet them."

Paranae said, "Thank you, Mr. Kim." She reached over and touched Mr. Park's hand. Mr. Park took her hand and held it on the way to Mr. Kim's apartment.

Mr. Kim called his wife and said Mr. Park needed to hide out for just a couple of hours and they would be coming over.

In Mr. Kim's apartment, his wife, Gina, had prepared some snacks and tea. The four of them sat down to watch the news. Mr. Kim and Gina spoke good English and Paranae enjoyed asking about their children who were in bed because it was late. Within moments, on the entertainment news, the story of what happened at the awards show came on. The news also showed large crowds around the hotel where Paranae was 'reportedly' staying at Mr. Park's apartment house.

Mr. Kim and his wife were visibly shocked. Mr. Kim said, "Mr. Park, you're not usually involved in scandals. Who is this lady?"

Mr. Park said, "I don't really know, but I do feel connected to her in some way. She said something to me that felt like a clue, that only a very few people would know about."

Mr. Kim said, "And so you kissed her?"

"She kissed me first!"

Three sets of eyes turned to Paranae.

"It's true that I also felt an immediate kinship with Mr. Park. He knows me from a book I wrote about him, and he knows of me from some contract negotiations at Netflix, but we've never actually met. Also, he doesn't know me by the name Paranae. I'm baffled too. Maybe we just have a natural affinity."

"It still seems weird to me," said Mr. Kim.

"When I first bumped into him, I said a keyword from my book that would get his attention. I'm sorry, Mr. Park."

"I'm not. It was great to meet you," he said.

"Scandal-wise, this will probably get a lot worse when they find out I'm forty years older than Mr. Park," Paranae said.

The three of them shouted simultaneously, "What?"

Tea was spilled and the kids woke up. Crying ensued. The parents jumped up and spent the next 30 minutes getting them back to sleep. One little girl wandered out and crawled into Mr. Park's lap. He just held her until she went back to sleep and then with the help of Mr. Kim carried her to bed. It seemed that Mr. Park had a lot of experience with kids.

While the parents were doing their final work with the children, Mr. Park and Paranae sat down on the couch. Paranae said, "Regarding that kiss you gave me backstage - it seemed pretty good. I myself am good at a lot of things in life, but I'm not so hot at kissing. Since you're a trained actor, maybe you could give me some quick training. Let me sit on your lap." Mr. Park marveled at the incredible natural boldness of Paranae and didn't object when she sat down on his lap.

"What about kissing on the cheek? Are there any special ways to do it? Any special lip formations?"

"I think the 'lip formation' is standard, pushed a little further out because the lips are not met by a counter set of lips," said Mr. Park. He said to himself, "Why am I treating this like it's some sort of legitimate conversation?"

"How does this look?" asked Paranae. "Can I try it out on your cheek?" He nodded.

She kissed his cheek and ended it with a loud smacking noise.

He put his hand up to cover his ear, "Why did you do that?"

"Wasn't that proper?" she asked.

"No."

"I'm such a slow learner! Now what about neck kisses?"

"Are you going to bite me like a vampire!?"

"If that's a part of my training," she said.

"No - it's not!"

"Maybe you should demonstrate things since you're so concerned. Start with neck kissing, with explanatory commentary."

"Okay, I will. In general, one might start out by staring at the other person's neck and then move aside any clothing that prevents access. Could you push your dress down off your shoulder?"

"Certainly." She did so as she raised one eyebrow and slightly pushed out her lips. Mr. Park shifted her body to have greater access to that side of her neck. His lips touched her shoulder, and she shivered. He looked up into her eyes and smiled. He put his arm behind her back and pulled her in a little closer. Then he lightly kissed the nape of her neck. She closed her eyes. He moved up her neck, pushed back her hair, and kissed behind her ear. His hair brushed against her cheek. Time seemed to stop. He pulled her even closer.

At that moment, Mr. Kim and Gina came back to the living room and were shocked by what they saw.

Mr. Park and Paranae broke apart and Paranae hopped off his lap.

"Mr. Park was just giving me some acting lessons," said Paranae.

Mr. Kim said, "It didn't look like acting to me."

"Back to our current scandal," said Paranae. "Should I leave the country by sea or by helicopter over to Japan?"

"Helicopter to Japan sounds good to me," said Mr. Park.

"Since Netflix brought me here, maybe someone from Netflix could go to my hotel room, get my bag and passport, arrange for a flight and any exit stamps and visa I may require, and send a person here to take me to the helicopter. I'll get on the phone and talk to my contact."

As they waited for the arrangements to be made, Paranae said, "You seem eager to get rid of me, Mr. Park."

"You're like a black hole sucking me in," said Mr. Park.

"More training while we wait?" asked Paranae. "Perhaps you could school us all on the fine art of handholding."

And so, for the next hour, the four of them sat on the sofa and went to other locations and practiced various hand-holding positions. Paranae would think what these positions could be, and Mr. Park would demonstrate with Paranae as a partner. Mr. Kim and Gina were partners. Some of the positions included: holding hands next to each other while seated on a couch; hiding hand-holding while seated on a couch; holding hands while walking; and hiding holding hands behind the back while standing. Paranae tripped and fell while walking and holding hands, causing Mr. Park to fall on top of her. Mr. Kim laughed while helping Mr. Park up. Paranae posed a dilemma while trying to hide both her hands behind her back. Mr. Park said, "Do you want me to handcuff you?" Mr. Kim and Gina giggled. Paranae's next request was to hold hands while jumping out of an airplane. Both couples held hands and jumped forward. Paranae yelled, "Geronimo."

Next was holding hands while one partner was dying in the hospital bed. Paranae insisted the dying partner had to really act like they were dying. First, she died, while Mr. Park held her hand. As she gasped loudly, she said to Mr. Park, "Husband of mine, I've left my millions to my lover, Jack." Even Mr. Park laughed at that. When Mr. Park was the dying partner, Paranae held his hand but slapped him several times with the other hand saying "Stay with me! Don't you go and die. We still have so many bills to pay!" Mr. Park grabbed her slapping hand and Paranae pondered, "Should I have slapped him harder?" Mr. Park took his opportunity and cried, "I'm dead, for God's sake!"

The next acting challenge was holding hands under dishwater. As Paranae went to the sink and filled it with water, Mr. Park pondered how the hell holding hands under dishwater could ever come to happen and asked the other couple to go first because he was out of ideas. Mr. Kim and Gina had a brief discussion, went to the freezer, and dumped a tray of ice into the sink. Then Mr. Kim grabbed his wife's wrist and exclaimed,

"You've burned your hand badly. Let's put it in this ice water," They plunged their hands into the water. Mr. Park and Paranae applauded.

Paranae then approached the sink, still full of ice water, found one of the kids' plastic sippy cups, took the lid off, and put the cup into the sink. "Most lovable husband, please come here for a minute." Mr. Park approached the sink. As he came close, Paranae picked up the cup filled with water and threw it in his face.

"What do you think you're doing?" he said. Meanwhile, Paranae was refilling the cup in the sink. She quickly threw another cup in his face. She put her hand back in the sink. Mr. Park rushed ahead and grabbed her hand in the sink. "Stop it!" "Let go of the cup!" She dropped it and Mr. Park grabbed her with both hands on her upper arms and pulled her away from the sink. At this point, Mr. Kim and Gina applauded. Mr. Park glared at them and then shook his head and wet hair all over Paranae's face, hair, and chest area. Then he let her go.

Paranae laughed and asked if they had any hand towels. Instead of drying herself off she went over and dried Mr. Park's face and hair as much as she could reach. She said, "You were a great impromptu actor and I'm sorry to be so mean."

"You should be sorry," he said as he dried her hair and face. He smiled at her for a moment. The two of them finished drying themselves off.

Mr. Kim and Gina were mystified by the whole drying-off exchange. It seemed like an interaction between two old friends or possibly even lovers.

Paranae was gung-ho for the game/training to continue. So, they held hands while crossing the street and avoiding traffic. Mr. Park was leading Paranae across the street when suddenly she got hit by a car or at least that's what Paranae said. The next exercise was holding hands in bed. Everyone lay down on the floor and did various handholds including one where one person rolled over on top of the other.

All four of them were laughing so loudly, they almost didn't hear the doorbell ring. They jumped up and let the driver in. Paranae hugged them goodbye, giving a much harder hug to Mr. Park, and said, "You are the greatest hand-holding trainer I've ever met."

After she left, the house became just so quiet. They all sat down on the couch and sighed. Mr. Park said, "What did she do to us? Are we all crazy?"

Gina said, "I loved it when she threw water in your face."

Mr. Kim said, "I loved it when she slapped you as you were dying, and you yelled 'I'm dead for God's sake."

They all laughed. And yet a tear ran down Mr. Park's cheek.

After I finished telling the story, Hae Jin looked at me for a while and said, "That was a great story." He kissed me gently and hugged me softly. I smiled. "Thank you for appreciating it."

Chapter 12
Age Discrimination Hits Martha Hard

I wanted to transform my story into some chalk drawings on the wall. First, we drew a stage with a big screen on the left side and red curtains on the right. Mr. Park even drew in a little host man in the middle. On another part of the wall, we worked on drawing Mr. Kim's nice, long blue sofa with a couple of decorative green pillows on it. The problem area to draw was backstage. It ended up looking like a long tunnel with dark curtains for walls and some stage lights hanging from the ceiling. A backstage cameraman stood about a third of the way from the stage. His camera was pointed toward the middle of the backstage area where Paranae and Mr. Park were to meet. Over the next few days, Hae Jin and Martha imagined the story until it became real to them.

Their next big chalk project was of South Korea. Hae Jin did this project by himself. First, he did a big outline of South Korea. Then he added some blue rivers and green mountain ranges. There were a lot of small islands to the west and south, which he dotted in, plus the bigger island of Jeju in the south. He put in cities and towns that he thought significant and had me pronounce each town a few times. Finally, he used dashes to indicate approximate provincial boundaries. He explained places he had been and where he liked to go. He described some of the food differences. He worked on it for three days.

I applauded and said, "If nothing else, you could become a South Korean geography teacher! Which island was the one where you were a vampire on *Busted?*"

"You watched that, too?"

"Yes. I loved it when you, as the island doctor, went out to examine the woman on the mountain who had been killed by a vampire. You confirmed that it looked that way to you. Immediately, instead of exclaiming the dangers of vampires to the crowd of villagers who were there, you asked them if they had had their flu shots yet. The villagers were great actors too and went along with you so calmly, like vampire killings were an everyday occurrence, but flu shots were special. That little segment showed some of your natural comic talent."

"Thank you, sweets," he said.

I sent him off to the shower and then to bed, where, after the chalky labors of the day, he slept soundly.

The next day, Hae Jin asked for a few packets of medium-sized post-its so we could use our maps as a training system. I didn't quite figure it out until a few days later when the post-its arrived. Then he excitedly resumed his professorial role with the South Korean map he had drawn. He put a post-it over each of the cities and towns that he had written on the map. There were about 30 of them. Then he asked me to name them. I would then pull the post-it off to see if I was right. 1 was only able to get four right or about 13%. The four I got right were Seoul, Incheon, Busan, and Jeju. To the side of the map, he created a little grid to record my progress. He then removed all the post-its, went over each name, and pronounced it again for me. He told me to spend some time studying the map and he would test me again tomorrow. This was irritating the hell out of me, but I saw how happy and motivated he seemed to be. Whatever I could do to keep his spirits up, I'd do. So, I sat in front of the map for 15 minutes at a time three times that day.

The next morning, he bounced up and dragged me over to the map.

"Hey," I said, "I haven't even gone to the bathroom or brushed my teeth. Plus, I need some wake-up tea!"

He conceded that that was true, and we both did our minimal morning prep to get back to the map. Standing at the wall, I tried again. I got seven right. He marked my score - the number correct

(7) and the percentage correct (23%). He looked disappointed. "This could take a while," he said. He took all the post-its off and repaired some of the chalk lines. (We needed some fixer spray for our chalk drawings, but the quantity needed for our small room full of chalk would probably kill us.) He then pronounced each and every town over again to me. "Please study this time."

"I studied the last time," I said.

"Well, I guess you are old, so maybe you have an excuse," he said in a pitying voice and with a pitying look.

At that point, I experienced something that I had only experienced once before with my husband: I literally saw red! After I'd had that experience with my husband, years ago, I said to myself that it would never happen again. My blood pressure must have shot up through the roof exploding some small capillaries in my eyes. This was a good way to have a stroke. I just broke my promise to myself and saw Hae Jin and the entire room in red.

I walked away to the bathroom, closed the toilet lid, sat down, and breathed in as much air as possible. Mr. Park peeked around the corner. "Stay away," I said. "I need to calm down." After a few minutes, it seemed as though I was getting dizzy, so I just lay down on the floor of the bathroom. The cool floor seemed to help.

Finally, Hae Jin came to sit on the bathroom floor. "I'm sorry," he said. "I struck out at you in the cruelest way. I know we've both struggled with our age difference, but to use this as a taunt against you is inexcusable. I'm not asking you to forgive me. I'm sorry. We have to decide in the midst of this totally unreal situation if we can be real people here. I think it will take courage. Are most people living with integrity and love? I so hope that we can."

"I've calmed down a little. Please help me sit up." Hae Jin put his arms around me.

"Your arms are even more comforting than your words. Thank you."

After standing up and walking around, we sat down by the mattress. "So, what happened to you?" Hae Jin asked. I explained to him that I actually 'saw red' and knew the dangers involved and that I had to calm down.

"As for why I got so mad, I can't quite pinpoint my reasons. Maybe I'm so afraid of losing you when others find out how old I am that I'm just blocking out that day. Maybe I'm scared of being old or being labeled 'old'. Maybe, no, definitely, I'm afraid of dying. I'm scared to leave you alone. Did all of that just coalesce in my head at that moment? Maybe I suddenly and completely doubted your love for me. I felt sick."

"Let's try not to be afraid. It's hard but be assured even our worst fears can be conquered together. It's not my love or your love, but our love. Let's not doubt our love as the powerful force it can be," said Hae Jin.

"I don't want you to think that your teaching methods are to blame either. Frankly, I thought what you did was brilliant. It may take me a few more study days for me to get the city names, but I will get them eventually. Maybe you could say the town name and a short fact or something that happened to you in that town, like "Busan, the city where I was born". That gives me something to tie the name to. I know many names of small towns in the Philippines through knowing something that happened there: like Dagupan, the town where MacArthur landed to take back the Philippines in World War II, or Tiwi, a town near Mount Mayon volcano."

"Let's try that. It sounds innovative and logical," he said. "Let me write down a phrase I can associate with each place." And so, I learned the name of each town over a three-week period.

Chapter 13
Roy Orbison Music; PHJ Proposes

My hair had grown out to a nice white fuzz and the stitches in my head had dissolved. Hae Jin had become proficient at braiding his hair. Our next chalk drawing was of a small café table under a tree in Provence. Sometimes we had wine and cheese at our table, at other times, we had coffee and croissants. We would have romantic talks about the universe or just about how handsome Hae Jin was. We drew a little pathway from there with stars and the moon in the sky to walk in at night. We would walk slowly down that path holding hands, remarking on how lucky we were to be able to see the sky. The tears in our eyes told the irony of those thoughts.

One day I asked Jin, as I now began to call him, if he had ever heard of the American singer Roy Orbison. He had! I was completely surprised. "Many of the songs are short-short stories about love and fear of loss of love, but where love wins out at the end. It would be so cool to be able to combine some great Korean talent, like you, with a classic American talent in the privacy of our own prison. Let's ask the guys up above to play a CD of his for us to sing and dance to."

The ceiling agreed with us and a couple of days later played a Roy Orbison CD. It became a regular afternoon feature. We would both dance around and reenact the stories in the songs as best we could. For *Cryin'*, I would walk slowly from one side of the room while he sang and walked toward me. He would smile at me tentatively. I said "hello" while holding his hand for a moment and then continued walking. Hae Jin would lean against our Buddha tree while tears streamed down his face. Sometimes, he would ham it up even more and sob at the end.

To do *Running Scared*, he would play two parts, the running scared one and the old arrogant boyfriend. For the running scared part, we started him in the shower looking very frightened and worried. The shower was running, his white hair streaming, his head against the wall, thinking and singing about his dilemma. Later, he and I would be strolling in a plaza and the ex-boyfriend would be standing in front of us. Hae Jin would walk over and play the boyfriend. The boyfriend was extremely handsome and confident. He smiled a dismissive smirk at the running scared one and glanced at me, raising his eyebrows as though to say, "Why are you with him, when you could have a magnificent person such as myself?" Hae Jin ran over to play Running Scared again, looking into my eyes. I smiled, linked arms with him, and we headed away in the opposite direction.

Falling was a difficult one for us to interpret. It's about a man who used a woman just for his own thrills. It's implied that the woman may have found out that he had just been pretending to love her. But while pretending to love her, he kissed her and fell in love with her. Now, it appears the woman is angry and about to desert him. He begs her to stay one more night and not to leave him now, just when he's falling in love with her. He begs her to say that she loves him. We decided to focus on the word falling, which comes up nine times. The second thing we came up with is that transformational kiss which changes him from a selfish jerk to a true lover. I wondered if Hae Jin could fall in nine different ways, and so he began to experiment. He fell forward with both arms extended above his head. He fell backward, he fell on his left side, and he fell on his right side. He fell on his butt; he fell on his knees. He did a broad jump and fell on his butt. We didn't count that one because he fell on his butt again. We put some padding on his face and his head, then had him fall on his face and fall on his head from a kneeling position. We only needed one more. Since we still needed that transformational kiss, we brilliantly came up with the idea of falling on his lips. His lips would fall on my lips for the transformational kiss. I lay down on the bed, and he hovered over me about 10 inches from my face, propped up by his arms, and had a controlled fall to my lips. It was certainly transformational and left me breathless. He whispered to me, "If you still love me, say that you love me." I whispered back, "I love you."

Another song we enjoyed was *You Got It*. Although it had an upbeat sound and possibly portrayed a man on a shopping spree, underneath was pure gratitude and thankfulness. It was a song of relief at being loved. All of these songs were sung by a man with an achingly beautiful voice, a voice that could convey pain and desperation as well as joy and love. What a voice! Even though some of our treatments may have seemed light or trivial, they were done with our love for each other and in appreciation of a great artist.

After our dances, Jin and I sat down on the mattress and leaned against the wall. "I've been thinking about the time when we get out of here, if we do get out," I said, "I will have overstayed my visa for a long time, and I won't even have my passport. I'll have to go to the American Embassy for a new passport, and I guess to the Korean Embassy for a new visa. Since the Korean Embassy won't know what I've been doing here for all this time, I may be deported. I'm not sure a person can come back to a country after they get deported."

"We can report our kidnapping to the police and show them this place," said Jin. "I'm famous in Korea, and they must know that I've been missing all this time. I will vouch for you."

"The kidnappers may take us far away, and we may never find out where 'this place' is. The embassy may not believe us. I don't know the laws on deportation here and I don't want to get you to do something you don't want to do, but if we were married, would that stop my deportation?"

"I don't know the laws either. I will hire the best lawyers to help you. Further, I've been thinking about asking you to marry me for a considerable time. Did you just beat me to the punch?"

Stunned, I said, "Why would you ever think of marrying me? What would your fans say? Wouldn't it affect your career?"

"You're the one who just brought it up! You just asked me to marry you to prevent your deportation! Wouldn't my fans be scandalized that I had been living with someone for months, and I didn't want to marry her? Is my career more important to me than you? I want to be with you. Quit fooling around and say you'll marry me."

"I don't want to be deported, because I don't want to be separated from you. Therefore, since it seems we agree, I will marry you, not because of deportation fears, but because I love you," with tears streaming down my face, "I'm not fooling." Hae Jin smiled.

"Let me ask once again so I can get a clear and definite answer." He knelt on the floor beside the mattress, held her hand, and said, "Martha, will you marry me?"

"Yes." We both smiled this time. Jin climbed up on the mattress and kissed me. We sat there for a while with our own thoughts.

"How much longer do you think that we and those up above can go on?" asked Jin.

"Are you eager to get married now that we're engaged?"

"Now that you mention it - yes," he said.

"It seems like they are friendly to us, they treat us pretty well. Get us things that we ask for, and cheer on our sexual encounters. Maybe they are on our side, maybe not. Let's ask them what we could do in order for them to decide to let us go."

"Why do they keep us here?" he asked.

"Maybe they are highly paid," I said.

"They seem to be interested in sex. Maybe we could exchange some spectacular sex show for our release."

"You wish! Let's ask them for a copy of the Kama Sutra, which may spark their interest and see what we can figure out."

Chapter 14
Measuring PHJ's Penis

Jin requested a copy of the Kama Sutra from the ceiling. A sort of buzz had been going on up above for a while during our marriage proposal discussion and continued at this request. A couple of days later our copy arrived, and we began to peruse it. It caused quite a few mystified looks between the two of us. The book we received was in English and although Mr. Park's English had improved greatly, I had to translate some of the racier sections.

"Let's go to the toilet area for this discussion. I think things could get a little too explicit," I said. "This chapter says that both men and women could be classified by the size of their private parts. For example, men's penises are basically small, medium, and large. Small is a hare; medium is a bull; and large is a horse. So why don't we look at yours and see what yours is?"

He jumped up and pulled down his pants.

Cautiously, I asked, "Before I say anything, what size would you say you are?"

He grabbed his dick, bent over, and began to examine it.

I smiled, "It seems to me that if you petted it just a little bit it might fall into a larger category."

"I bet you're right about that," he said while performing a bit of petting. Of course, it got a lot bigger and straighter, too.

My eyes widened, "I'm going to risk a guess and say that you're a bull.

The translation session ended suddenly, but a Kama Sutra practice session began...

Later, I re-read (several times) the classification of the size of the vagina so I could better explain it to Mr. Park. "I'm really baffled at how the determinations of the size or depth of the vagina were made. It implies to me that men went out and had sex with various animals and then had sex with various human females until it was determined that a small vagina (or 'yoni' as they call it) was comparable to that of a deer. The middle-deep yoni made the woman a mare, and a really deep yoni made her an elephant. There are two other factors to consider; the passion she exhibits during sex and the time it takes her to come."

"You're kidding, right?" asked Mr. Park.

I shook my head no. I continued, "First, I must ask: Does your penis go all the way in when we're having sex?"

"Yes, I would say so," he said.

"I think we may need a ruler. Let's get your penis to its maximum length and then we can measure it."

"You are diabolical!" he exclaimed in a kind of admiring way.

"We don't have to do it right this second and we need the ruler first," I said.

Hae Jin yelled up at the ceiling, "Hey guys, we need a ruler to measure my penis!"

Literally, it sounded like a whole tray of dishes dropped on the floor up above us. We smiled at each other.

"In the broader sense, or the longer your penis is, the more able you'll be able to perform the spectacular sex event that may set us free," I said.

"Why? Have you read something spectacular?" he asked.

"I'm still trying to get my mind around it, but it will also require a lot of endurance from you. In other words, you're going to have to keep it up for a long period of time while either you or I maneuver around it."

He seemed thoughtful, "I think I have pretty good endurance. What do you think?"

"Why do you think I'm so exhausted all the time?" I smiled. "Anyway, the 'sex event' I'm thinking of will require a lot of athletic ability and may require a few practice sessions under the cover of darkness, I suppose."

"Practice sounds good," he said, smiling.

"I'll keep reading the book and see if there are any chapters on endurance. There is a chapter on thickening the penis, mainly by using sandpaper to scar the penis and thereby thickening it."

Instinctively, Mr. Park covered his private parts with his hands and screamed. I tried to approach him, but he just backed away with a horrified look on his face and with his hands stubbornly planted on the threatened zone.

The heavens parted and a ruler fell from the ceiling.

"That was quick," I said. "Let's go someplace private, to our camera-free zone, to measure your dick - to the toilet."

As we marched to the toilet, I said to Hae Jin that we may have to talk a bit louder in the toilet area so everyone could hear.

Ensconced in the toilet area, I said, "First, we must measure it in its natural state to get the resting measurement. Please remove your pants."

"Only after you remove yours," he said loudly and defiantly.

"Glad to oblige. Now I will grab your penis and stretch it out lightly to get a pre-expansion reading."

"Ow, that doesn't seem like 'stretching it out lightly' to me!"

I gave him a little 'sorry' kiss on his penis. "Anyway, our official reading of your relaxed penis is________ (which, I whispered in his ear). That is quite sizable right now! What will we have to do to make it stand up on its own?"

"What about some tried and true techniques we have used in the past?"

"Such as?" I asked.

"Such as kissing, licking, and you know - I love ping-pong," he said.

"I guess I'll have to warm my mouth up a bit then," I said. I started making some lip-smacking and slurping sounds.

The entire ceiling shook.

I proceeded to apply kissing and licking to the designated area and Hae Jin began to respond with a dreamy look on his face. When he was about half-way up, I played a sort of hand ping-pong using his penis as the ping-pong ball. His penis was astoundingly (to me) lengthy by this time.

I said, "Hand me the ruler quick. Hold your dick steady while I get a measurement."

I measured it and whispered the result to Hae Jin. He tossed aside the ruler, pulled off my shirt, lifted me up until I could brace my feet on the toilet, and we proceeded to have sex against the wall.

We stumbled out of the toilet area, went to the shower, and showered together. After dressing, we sat down with our backs against the mattress and Mr. Park began negotiations with our captors for our release.

"Hello, people up above us. We have become aware that you seem to be interested in our sexual encounters. We have found in the Kama Sutra book an outstanding sexual session that will astound you. We are willing to try it if you will release us. Our release must be with both of us alive and uninjured. Please think about this and respond as soon as possible."

I showed Hae Jin the passages in the Kama Sutra which described some unbelievable sex acts. He said that these sex acts were not only unbelievable but completely undoable. One position, which I named "the twirl", involved the man doing a 360-degree turn while inside on top of the woman. The other one, while slightly more doable, I named "the wall". This placed the man next to a wall, the woman suspended on his linked hands with her thighs and calves doubled up on his chest while the woman controlled the sex by pushing on the wall behind the man with her toes. I said I had been thinking about them and that I had devised some specially designed clothing that would cover up our private parts. I showed him the diagrams I had made in my little notebook.

"Do you think they would be satisfied with all this elaborate cover-up by your costumes? You might as well just put us in hijabs or how about under a tent!"

"I'm trying to preserve some privacy - dignity - something. Let me think some more," I said.

"Let's admit it there is no privacy or dignity in this whole idea! We can't do this. Do you think we can trust our kidnappers not to secretly film us? Are they so noble by keeping us imprisoned all this time? What about us? Even without the filming, are you willing to do this in front of some unknown number of people or should I say perverts and scumbags? Won't we know what we did for the rest of our lives? Wouldn't we just begin to hate ourselves and each other? I'm not doing it, and neither are you! If necessary, let's just die together!"

Hae Jin's body was literally trembling, vibrating. Tears streamed down his face. I sat on the floor and cried, "I just don't know what to do." Hae Jin came to me, extended his hand, stood me up, embraced me, and said, "Let's just die together."

A few minutes later, I stepped back and said, "Dying doesn't appeal to me."

Hae Jin smiled and then laughed.

I said, "Let's just rescind our previous proposal and ask them if they can't just let us go. If they say no, let's live our lives here for as long as we can. I can't bear to part with you right now."

Hae Jin said to the ceiling, "We retract our latest proposal. Please consider releasing us soon, you must be tired of this."

We made some dinner, ate, and sang some songs. Later we went to bed and slept until morning.

Chapter 15
Getting Released; Imprisonment Was Streamed!

An announcement came from above, "Your proposal to be released has been accepted. It will take us a day to remove all our equipment. You will be hearing lots of loud noises as we move things around. Do not be alarmed. Tomorrow you will be released."

Not knowing what to do or say, we decided to do our exercises, take showers, and get on with our day. We ate our breakfast at the chalk drawing of a café table in France. "It sounds like we're going to be released right here. I'd like to preserve this room, spray fixer on all the chalk sections, and make it a mini-museum or a private property for us to view occasionally. I don't want the police to mess it up," said Hae Jin.

"We can explain that to the police and any forensic people they send in. Certainly, they can take good photographs for evidence preservation purposes. Later, we may be able to use those photos to repair any damage to the walls. I've even seen photos printed on large silk screens to do tours of famous paintings without the actual paintings. What do you think of asking for a couple of black silk outfits, turtlenecks, and pants to go well with our white hair to wear out tomorrow? Maybe we will need shoes too."

Hae Jin shouted our last request to the boys upstairs and they called back "Okay."

"Do you think we can go to your apartment tomorrow?"

"I hope so if the police can keep this under wraps. It may end up being like your Paranae story from before: we may have to flee from the press."

The rest of the day we just chatted away like school kids about to get out for vacation. It still seemed so unimaginable to us. After dinner, a plastic bag dropped from the ceiling with our new clothes. We tried them on, and they seemed so perfect for us. Hae Jin looked like a beautiful eccentric artist, and I looked like a decent-looking older woman. Hae Jin said, as we looked in the bathroom mirror, that we looked like a real couple. He wiped away my tears before they messed up my blouse and asked, "Why are you crying?"

"Did you think we might not look like a 'real couple'?"

"Never. We're probably 'realer' than any other couple! Now let's get this outfit off of you." We hung up our clothes and went to bed, exhausted for some reason.

In the morning, we woke up to a voice from above. "We will proceed with your release, but it will take us about an hour to completely vacate the building. After we leave, we will trigger the opening of a door. Please get dressed and move the mattress to the side of the room near the entrance to the bathroom. This is for your safety. Stay seated on the mattress as a large door will fall open on the opposite side of the room. Although you may not believe us, it's been our pleasure being with you. Goodbye."

We washed up in the bathroom and put on our black outfits. Hae Jin combed and braided his hair. He looked the most handsome I had ever seen him. My hair was long enough to look like a man's haircut. Hae Jin fiddled with combing my hair and arranging it. He said, "You look the most beautiful I've ever seen you."

We went to the bedroom, slid the mattress to the designated location, and sat and waited. We held hands and smiled. My heart was pounding. "Now that the day has come, do you think we'll make it in the outside world?"

"Let me do a little reconnoitering as we leave to see if things are on the up and up. I'll keep within sight of you. I'll ask someone to get the police."

The room went completely dark. The air in the room stopped moving. Suddenly, a part of the wall about the size of a garage door creaked open and fell outward loudly to the ground. A cloud of dust came at us. Standing up, coughing, and running into some fresh air was our priority. We cleared the dusty area and found that we were inside a large warehouse. Dusting ourselves off, I said, "So much for our spiffy new clothes." We shook our hair out too, and then we smiled. We saw a small door near what looked like larger doors for big vehicles.

"Do you think the doors are locked?" we both said simultaneously. We walked to the small door and surprisingly it opened! Stepping through the door, we could see the warehouse was at the bottom of a small hill. At the top of the hill, about two blocks away, we could see people walking by. Hae Jin said, "Stay right here. Stand inside the doorway so no one will be able to see you, but you can still see me. I'll go talk to someone up there and have them call the police."

Mr. Park started walking up the hill, but near the top of the hill, people started to notice him and ran toward him. They yelled, "It's Park Hae Jin!" Hae Jin was tempted to run and recoiled from the crowd coming toward him, however they quickly surrounded him.

"Wait, how did you recognize me so quickly? I don't look like Park Hae Jin."

"Yes, you do! You even have your new black outfit on."

"What? Are you, my kidnappers? If not, please call the police."

Someone said they were calling the police right now. One of the women in the crowd said, "But where's Martha?"

At this, Hae Jin became so alarmed he tried to push his way through the crowd. Finally, two guys just held him by his arms as he struggled.

One of the guys said, "Calm down, Mr. Park. We're not your kidnappers. We know about you because your captivity has been streamed on the internet for many months now. We saw you two last night trying on your outfits."

Just then, police officers came running through the crowd, telling everyone to break it up. Hae Jin was just trying to take in what the crowd had said about internet streaming. The police officers stopped in their tracks. "It's Park Hae Jin!" The crowd laughed. The policemen looked around at the crowd and the same officer said, "But where is Martha?" The crowd laughed even harder.

I couldn't stand it anymore and was walking up the hill and stood behind the crowd. "I'm right here. Let go of Park Hae Jin." The crowd parted and Hae Jin came to me. "It's okay, Martha. These people know about us because apparently our captivity has been streamed all over the internet." Suddenly, the crowd surrounded both of us and started snapping photographs with their phones and asking for autographs. The police made calls for backup.

I, speaking in English with a few Korean words thrown in, said, "It's not all right for you to take our pictures without our permission. If you've watched us for months, then you should know! Officers control these people! As the first people to find us, we will allow you to take a picture with us, individually or as a group. After that, you must leave in an orderly manner. Officers, do not allow any other people to come down here." Hae Jin translated it into proper Korean and said he completely agreed. More police officers arrived and blocked the road at the top of the hill. The people lined up and took selfies with Hae Jin and me. We shook each person's hand and asked them not to say anything about us to the people gathering at the top of the hill beyond the police line. The crowd moved up the hill and through the police line.

Higher-ranking police officers came down the hill. Hae Jin explained that he wanted the scene preserved, that none of the chalk drawings be erased, and that photographs of all the walls be taken. After that, Hae Jin and I led them to the warehouse, telling them that flashlights would be needed. As they gazed at the room and the platform up above, the police captain called for forensics and further backup. Leaving the warehouse behind, a discussion began about where we should go and what transportation would be needed to get us there. Some of the ideas presented included PHJ's apartment, his sister's place, friends' houses, the Korean Embassy, the American Embassy, a 5-star hotel, a yacht, and a police station located far from this location.

Hae Jin asked for a phone and called his sister. She screamed and cried for a while until Hae Jin calmed her down. He asked her what she thought about them coming over to her house. She said that enough security couldn't be provided and that she would soon be a target for reporters too. She asked if I was there with him. Hae Jin handed the phone to me. I said hello and that I was looking forward to meeting her someday. Mr. Park's sister said, "Thank you so much for being there with him."

Meanwhile, the police captain was speaking with the police commissioner. The police commissioner, not hearing of this until now, was momentarily frozen. When he thought for a moment, he said," Bring them in an unmarked police car to police headquarters. Have two other unmarked cars convoy with them. No sirens."

"Please get us somewhere quickly, because I must go to the bathroom," I said.

Hae Jin smiled. "If she says she needs to go, she needs to go. Let's put a police hat and jacket on her and have a couple of cops or maybe four cops escort her to a bathroom up on the street. Right now!"

I, in my disguise, went up the hill and into a store that had a bathroom just in the nick of time. Sauntering back down the hill, I gave a thumbs-up sign to Hae Jin and the captain. As I reached them, the police line opened and a black car came down the hill and picked up Hae Jin, me, and the police captain. At the top of the hill, another black car went out in front of them, and a black car followed them. I looked at the streets of Seoul and marveled since it was my first look. Both I and Hae Jin stared at the trees and sky, "Wow."

Since I still had on my police disguise, the captain threw a blanket over Hae Jin's head and shoulders and escorted him up to the commissioner's office. I joked, "Who knew I would become a policeman when I grew up?" The men in the room laughed.

The police commissioner had been busy since he gave the orders to bring them to his office. Seated in the room were the Korean Ambassador and the American Ambassador. They quickly introduced themselves. Hae Jin and I sat down, and I removed my police hat. The police captain remained standing. Another police officer entered the room, spoke to the commissioner, and then turned on the television. One of the persons who had helped them, in the beginning, was showing the picture he had taken with Hae Jin and me to a reporter and pointing down the block where a police line was established to protect the warehouse they had emerged from.

The captain said, "We need more officers to protect the warehouse which is a crime scene," and walked out of the room.

"Why don't Martha and I go on TV at a press conference and ask people to not interfere with the police at the crime scene in order to protect the evidence that might be found about our kidnappers?" asked Hae Jin.

The Korean Ambassador said, "I could join them along with the commissioner and the American Ambassador and assure them that we are trying to work through any legal concerns or difficulties and also to get you to a place of safety right now."

"Why are guys like you getting involved like this? Is it really such a big deal?" I asked.

The American Ambassador answered, "You two are the most famous people in the world right now and will probably soon be a couple of the richest."

"Well, I'm glad for your vote of confidence on our financial prospects, but I think we might want to do this virtually and then relocate again quickly because I'm sure that many of your embassy drivers and staffers know where you are and will track us down quickly when they see you appearing with us," said Hae Jin. "You probably know some rich business owner or big entertainment company who could put us up at their vacation home. We'll need some security and personal assistants to feed and clothe us also, but not too many. Please arrange a place for us to go. Commissioner, arrange some non-descript vehicles to get us there and maybe some decoy vehicles also, please. Once this is all ready, let's hold the press conference and then leave immediately."

About 20 reporters showed up for the conference, not really knowing what it was about. The Commissioner, the Ambassadors, Hae Jin, and I were in a separate room that transmitted our images to the conference room. The Commissioner and the Ambassadors introduced themselves to the reporters. The Commissioner stated, "We have a situation right now that needs the help and cooperation of every citizen in Korea. You may have heard from the news stations and the internet that Park Hae Jin and Martha Karr were released from their imprisonment this morning. This is true." The reporters began to type furiously on their computers and to film what was being presented to them on the screen at the front of the room. "The warehouse where they were held may contain vital evidence against their kidnappers. Please do not attempt to enter that warehouse or interfere with an ongoing police investigation or you will be arrested. Park Hae Jin and Martha Karr will now speak to you on this concern."

The conference room became quiet as the camera showed me and Hae Jin. Hae Jin then spoke, "Martha and I are going someplace where we can hide. We are going from one prison to another kind of prison. We will be safe and well. Don't worry about us. Let's try to develop other ways for fans to be fans and reporters to be reporters. When you are crowding around us, following us, screaming at us - you don't make us happy, and you don't make yourselves happy either. Let's start to find more respectful ways to treat each other. We'd like to be able to walk among you as fellow human beings. If you see a crowd forming around a celebrity, remind yourself that it's not your time to join that crowd. Maybe you'll see us some other time. It's okay to admire us but take time to develop your own lives, not dependent upon seeing a celebrity up close. Be prouder of loving your wife and kids, your mom and dad, and your co-workers. I don't think you want to have inscribed on your tombstone that in 2023 you saw Park Hae Jin in a parking lot as though that was the most important thing in your life. Martha and I love all of you who truly care and are concerned. Please enjoy your day today." The screen went blank. The reporters applauded briefly and then frantically began to call in their stories.

Hae Jin and I walked quickly to a van in the rear of the police station and traveled for about an hour to a home in the mountains. Our room was big and bright with clean white sheets on the bed. After showers, we found some matching pajamas to put on, went downstairs to the kitchen, and met the cook. The cook had prepared a great meal, which we ate while watching the news on TV. We discovered a couple of cell phones on the table.

The news frankly shocked us. Demonstrations and celebrations were held for us all over Korea, the United States, Japan, China, India, Australia, the UK, and Kenya. In fact, it seemed to be all over the world! Policemen were being interviewed, the Commissioner, and the Ambassadors, too.

I said, "I guess we're moving to Antarctica." A little later I said, "We need an executive secretary, an accountant, a lawyer, and a security firm." Hae Jin nodded wearily. He said, "I'll call my agent, accountant, and lawyer and get them working on the problem right away. After that, though, I want to just take a couple of days for us to be together, relax, and practice some of those Kama Sutra moves."

We found a note from the Police Commissioner saying the phones were "clean". We pretended like we knew what that meant and decided to use them. Hae Jin called his agent first.

His agent asked, "Where are you?"

Hae Jin said, "I don't know, but I'm safe."

His agent said, "You're currently receiving offers as well as monetary gifts from all over the world. What do you want to do?"

"Please compile a running list of offers and gifts and have our lawyers check if everything is ethical and legal every few days, as I think this is going to keep going for a while. Text me the list every time you update it. Coordinate money coming in with my accountant. Also, check that your phone isn't bugged before you call or text me."

"Okay. Maybe we'll form a little task force over here," said his agent.

"On another topic, Martha and I would like to get married soon. I'll be discussing this with her and giving you the details soon."

"Congratulations, boss." Hae Jin hung up.

I looked inquisitively at him.

Hae Jin said, "I think we need to do this before things get too hectic. I hope you remember that you said yes."

Chapter 16
Got Married. Did the Kama Sutra

"I remember. I also think we should get married as soon as possible to just calm down further speculation. Some people may be for us getting married and some may be against us. But once it's a fait accompli, I think they can begin to move on. We should probably have the wedding filmed to later verify that it did happen."

"You and I are thinking along the same lines. Why don't we just have it in the backyard here, have guests brought in large limos with black tinted windows, have our hosts provide some food and drinks, and later we'll say goodbye to them?" asked Hae Jin.

"We need to bring in people a couple of times ahead of time to measure, design, and fit our wedding outfits. Then on the day of the wedding, we need people to do makeup, and we need a film crew. There are lots of possibilities for information leaks, so we may once again have to leave this location and go to another location for our honeymoon."

"Are you already thinking about our honeymoon?" he asked.

"I wasn't really, since it seems like we've been on our honeymoon for a long time. But, now that I'm thinking about it, I wonder if it will be any different. Will you be even more handsome? More fun? More loving? We have so many more tasks ahead of us. I find that I'm becoming so ambitious for us to actually work together on things and make decisions together. I want to do so much together with you right now. I have so many ideas."

"I'm feeling ambitious right now too. That's a good way to put it. If we really have a lot of money we could produce shows, plays, and music videos. We could help so many people, we could travel, but let's concentrate on getting married for right now."

"I'm assuming your sister, and any other female relatives you wish to invite, will need to be fitted for a new gown also."

"I'll contact my agent and my sister to make arrangements. I have several friends I'd like to invite, too. Is there anyone you'd like to invite?"

"I'd like to invite the friend here in Korea whom I originally came to see. I'd also like to invite the main cast members and their spouses from *Man to Man* since that was where I first saw you."

Two weeks later Park Hae Jin and I were married in the backyard of someone's house. The Police Commissioner provided extra security and a get-away convoy for us to our next location. The two ambassadors performed the ceremony. Park Sung Woong graciously hosted the event. I had on a simple gown with a black lace top, to disguise any strange acting up by my breasts, and a white skirt. I wanted to remind others, and be reminded myself, of the escape costumes from our time of captivity when we had fallen in love. Hae Jin looked stunning. He had shaved his beard but still had his long white hair which swirled around him in the light breeze. As I approached him to say our vows and exchange rings, tears streamed down his face. I stepped up to him and wiped the tears away. The crowd made a moaning sound. I stepped back. We said our vows, were pronounced married, and kissed with our eyes wide open. We wanted to see the moment. We held both our hands together and smiled at each other. Finally, the clapping and cheering from the crowd got our attention as we turned to greet them.

Many photos were taken of the wedding party. I got to meet the cast members of *Man to Man* and proposed a spin-off with all the same cast members but in different roles. I wanted to call it *Woman to Woman*. They laughed at the idea, but some were intrigued. The new couple cut the cake, fed each other very neatly (to the disappointment of the crowd), had a sip of champagne, and danced briefly. I and Hae

Jin went inside to change into our traveling clothes. Hae Jin braided his hair, which kept his hair from being coated in frosting. Park Sung Woong and Jeong Man Sik captured Hae Jin as the couple came back outside, while I put a pile of frosting onto his nose. I said, "My, what a big nose you have." Hae Jin got free, grabbed me, wiped the frosting off with one hand, and rubbed it all over my lips. He said, "What frosty, sweet lips you have!" and began to lick the frosting off my face and lips. The audience clapped and cheered him on. I fought back by kissing him several times and rubbing some of the frosting on him. A truce was soon declared, and wet towels were brought to clean our faces. After that, we went around to everyone to thank them for coming. At the microphone, Hae Jin said that he hoped to be able to see them soon and work on other projects with them. "We are hoping the entire video of our wedding will be shown soon on a TV show and that you will each receive some good publicity out of this. We also hope that Martha and I can better normalize our situation and become more able to be with our fans and with society soon. Right now, though, we are relocating and going on our honeymoon."

With that, Hae Jin and I walked through the house to a waiting car that had our luggage and took us to a nearby small airport. From there we flew to a small island and another beautiful house. Hae Jin walked onto the porch, opened the front door, picked me up, slammed the door behind him with his foot, went upstairs, found the master bedroom, and threw me on the bed. He removed his clothes, then he removed my clothes, then went to the bathroom for coconut oil and a couple of towels. I said, "Dearest husband, you seem to be rather intensely in a hurry." "Dearest wife, I am." But after that, we began to take their time. Thus began one of the most memorable days of our lives. If only we could press together hard enough, long enough. We wanted to become one - and for some moments it seemed as though we had.

Hae Jin had arranged that the house and grounds be completely empty for three days with pre-prepared food and snacks, oils, towels, robes, swimsuits, beach wear, and anything else the house staff thought that the newlyweds might want. Some security was there but at a great distance. Nudity became prevalent in the house and pool area. The house was a beachfront property, so at night we sat on the beach and actually saw the stars and moon, which we had only previously drawn in chalk. Experimental beach sex left us sandy, but we had brought a large beach towel which kept the sand out of key parts. We showered off in the poolside shower. Donning some beach clothing, we went to the living room couch to talk about the next day.

"I think I set a new world record for the number of female orgasms in any one day," I said. Hae Jin said, "I think I set a new world record for the number of hours erect in one day." We smiled at each other proudly.

"Since we proved our stamina and agility today, maybe we could tackle those two Kama Sutra positions which seemed impossible before, as well as embarrassingly exhibitionistic, tomorrow."

Well-rested, we went to the living room the next morning. I said, "One of our previous problems, as I considered doing this in captivity, was designing clothing to cover private body parts. We don't have that obstacle now. Let's put down some blankets, sheets, and pillows on the and do 'the twirl' right here."

"Since you have thought this through more thoroughly than I have, will there be other problems?"

"The torso and legs on both of us would need plenty of oil to permit your body to slide on top of my body. Our private parts would also need copious amounts of oil, much more than usual. The main problem, as far as I can figure it, is the angle of entry. The closer you could get your dick to a right angle in relationship to the floor, the more likely you could do 'the twirl'. Think of a top spinning on the ground. It implies to me that the woman would have to be as athletic as the man."

"What are you talking about?" asked Hae Jin.

"Just keep listening for a while and see if you begin to understand. My hips would have to be elevated for your member to be at 90° to the floor while inside. However, the more my hips are elevated, the more my thighs and knees would block you. Therefore, my legs would have to be flat and out to the sides."

I got a couple of pillows from the couch, put them on the floor, and sat on the floor with my thighs on the pillows. I leaned back and put my head and shoulders on the blankets thus elevating my midsection. Then I brought my knees up perpendicular to the floor, dropped my knees to the sides, and placed the bottom of my feet together.

"Hop on, add some coconut oil, and start! You're going to have to be slightly elevated yourself to work your way around, sort of like a crab."

Hae Jin, completely ready, climbed on and in, but because of the sharp bend in my back, his beginning location resulted in his chest being in my face. He pushed up his torso to avoid suffocating me and understood why he had to support himself this way. I placed one hand on his back as the Kama Sutra instructed. He slowly began to turn his body to the left, but that slow movement was driving me crazy, and I started coming. Hae Jin paused and tried to be as still as possible while I had a conniption fit. About 1/8 of the way, I exploded again and my hand, on his back, became claw-like until I could settle down and breathe normally. I had another occurrence at 3/8's of the way. Hae Jin's eyes were crossing. Finally, at halfway, Hae Jin shot off and I joined him. Hae Jin fell to one side of the pillows, and I doubled over on the other side.

Hae Jin finally said, "I see why the Kama Sutra said this needs a lot of practice to be able to do this. My dick feels smashed."

"I think I'm now in the 'elephant' category," I said, as I started to laugh. I crawled over to Jin, kissed him, and said, "Good effort." He laughed too.

"I was actually amazed that you made it that far," I said.

"You were amazed?! I was astounded! I thought the bottom half of my body was going to explode," said Hae Jin. He suddenly lay back and fell asleep on the floor. I smiled and fell asleep beside him.

We woke up a couple of hours later in a tangle of oily sheets and blankets. These were taken to the laundry room and dumped on the floor. Showers were next and then we ate a giant lunch.

For the rest of the day, we took it easy. We established an easy pace. We only had sex three times - once in the pool, once on the beach, and once in bed. We decided to suspend efforts on 'the twirl' indefinitely.

Chapter 17
Appear on Men on a Mission Show

The next day, the third day, we had set aside for discussions about future actions interspersed with some "personal care" breaks. The first item that came up was to pursue an investigation into compensation from the streaming service that had profited from our imprisonment. Secondly, Hae Jin stated that a full discussion with his agents and agency about future filming prospects and projects was needed. He had spent his adult life as an actor, he enjoyed it and needed to continue acting in any way he could. A full financial picture was needed, but we thought there would be plenty of money to do almost anything we wanted to do. Hae Jin wanted to buy, possibly through contributions, the warehouse where our chalked-up room was and create a mini-museum. Other ideas he had for the warehouse included a stage for theater productions or concerts at one end and places for action movie scenes at the other end.

I wanted to produce a *Woman to Woman* follow-up for *Man to Man*. I also wondered if Hae Jin could make a video using Roy Orbison's music. I wanted to visit all my friends in Southeast Asia and most of all to go to Kenya to introduce Hae Jin to the Maasai people. I hoped we could spend a couple of months there. One question was, now that we were married, should we adopt children? Could the children be Hae Jin's biological children through in vitro fertilization and surrogate mothers? How long would I live to get a chance to be their mother?

I said to Jin, "Children could be good companions for you after I'm gone. You'll be young enough to marry again if you want to."

Hae Jin broke down as I talked about the inevitable conclusion to our relationship. But wasn't it the inevitable conclusion to each marriage and each life?

I said, "Remember your talk to me about living with courage and without fear? The only way we can do this is through our love."

"But what about grief? What will I do about grief?" asked Hae Jin.

"Grief is a part of loving the dead and is a part of loving yourself, of honoring your love. So, embrace it when it comes. Practice smiling. You're the strong one here. Don't forget that. You've got guts. You just married a woman 35 years older than you!"

Hae Jin laughed through his tears.

The staff and security came in for the next four days of our honeymoon. It was fun to interact with them. Hae Jin's and my private life continued in our bedroom.

We decided to try to normalize our situation by moving back to Hae Jin's apartment with a slightly increased security staff. We realized we would probably need security for the rest of our lives. We registered our marriage with the government. To better deal with fans, we planned a monthly Zoom meeting with them. We bought a larger apartment in Malaysia and decorated it together. We sponsored a meeting in Bali with all my friends. I contacted my former husband's cousin to attend a cultural training program for two months with the Maasai in Kenya. I went ahead with my plan of re-doing *Man to Man* into *Woman to Woman,* I met with lawyers, writers, cast, and crew members. Within nine months, the new K-drama finished production with the same cast, but with virtually everyone in different roles. Kim Min-Jeong was now Guard Kim, Park Sung Woong was the Doha character with a different name, and Park Hae Jin was Ungwang. These stars were invited to a *Men on a Mission* broadcast.

All of the *Men on a Mission* cast came out and did their regular pre-guest jokes. Finally, Park Sung Woong, Kim Min-Jeong, Chae Jung-An, Jung Man-Sik, and Park Hae Jin came in as being from the School of Acting Smart.

Ho-dong welcomed them all. The MOAM guys all knew Park Sung Woong and Chae Jung-An from previous appearances on the show and many of them now spoke to them. The three newer ones were singled out and introduced by Ho-dong. He particularly welcomed Park Hae Jin and said he was glad to see him looking so well after his recent ordeal. A period of talking about each star's 'Application for Admission' was conducted by Soo-geum. Park Hae-Jin's qualifications were discussed last, and he said he had brought a video that had never been seen before on TV and would MOAM like to be the first to air it?

"What is it a video of?" asked Soo-geum.

"It's a video of my marriage to Martha Karr with all the cast of *Woman to Woman* in attendance."

The MOAM were stunned and then overjoyed to see it. The video showed the backyard wedding and Park Hae Jin with his long white hair. Everyone exclaimed it was a beautiful wedding. They asked a bunch of questions. Since all the guest cast members had attended the wedding, they each made comments and answered questions. Finally, Hae Jin said, "If you wouldn't mind meeting someone who helped write *Woman to Woman,* saved my life, and married me, I'd like to introduce Martha Karr."

I then opened the sliding door and walked into the classroom. I smiled and went to stand by Hae Jin. I said, "Wasn't he lovely with his long white hair?"

All of the MOAM and even the cameramen and support staff stood up. Jang-Hoon walked to the front, bowed, shook Hae Jin's and my hands, and said congratulations. Each of the other men came forward, bowed, shook our hands, and said congratulations. Hae Jin said, "Well, I didn't know you would react so formally. Thank you. Everyone please, take a seat."

I, speaking in Korean, said, "First of all I don't speak Korean that well and I wonder if Yeong-Cheol could do some translating, if necessary, thus relieving Hae Jin of that burden. Furthermore, since I'm way older than any of you, I'm not going to use honorifics, if that's okay." Switching to English, I said, "Yeong-Cheol would you mind coming up here and standing by me?" He immediately came to the front, "Are there any questions?"

Jang-Hoon asks, "We know you were kidnapped - do you know who did it yet?"

Hae Jin answered, "No but the police and the NIS are looking into it. We weren't physically harmed by our captors unless you count our lack of freedom and my hair turning white. However, we were held in a small, windowless space for several months, afraid of what might happen to us. We are receiving counseling."

I spoke up, "I don't think I was originally intended to be kidnapped with Mr. Park. I got swept up accidentally. No telling what would have happened if I hadn't been there. Laughing and playing together got us through."

Sang-min asked, "You've been married for several months now. How would you say it's going?"

Hae Jin held my hand, "She's an amazing person. To be able to love someone in freedom is a little different than when we were in captivity. The desperation we felt before, we still feel. But in the midst of that desperation is a deep trust that we've developed, and that trust creates a connection between us that's hard to explain. It's as though that connection springs from deep in the earth."

I said, "He's a beautiful creation of the universe and impossible not to love. We're doing fine."

Heechul then asked, "I've heard that some of Hae Jin's fans are not happy with this marriage and are giving you both a hard time on the internet."

I said, "They shouldn't deprive themselves of being a fan of his. I am 75 years old. I won't be around forever. I may die in just a few years, then (addressing the camera) you may wish to resume your thoughts of loving Park Hae Jin. We both think no one should spend their lives angry and unhappy. We certainly love even those who are angry right now because we know there is a hurt behind that anger. Please consider your own lives and live as happily as you can."

Hae Jin added, "Martha would like to leave me with some children that are my own biological children. So, I'm asking if any of my female fans between the ages of 25 and 30 would be willing to become a surrogate mother for a child that Martha and I could raise. This would involve many things on the fan's part-including going through a rigorous screening process, being medically and mentally fit, being pregnant for nine months, and giving the baby up shortly after birth. Many legal papers would need to be signed giving me custody of the child. If possible, we would like to have one child this year and one child two years from now, preferably not from the same person. The mother would be given medical, housing, and financial aid during the time of pregnancy, as well as a trust fund for the rest of her life. As of today, there are forms on my website if you wish to apply. I have formed a team of lawyers and doctors to oversee this process. If no one applies, so be it. Martha and I will adopt children. We will be the best parents we can be."

Soo-geum said, "That seems to be a monumental announcement on our show today. I hope people will be understanding of your situation."

Ho-Dong said, "You all have passed, let's go to the school theater."

In the theater, we split up into two teams. The point of the game they played was to identify a K-drama from a brief scene description. Everyone was surprised that I got a lot of the answers correct. Finally, my team won, and my team received some giant Korean pork packages. I exclaimed, "This is great, but I think the head of the losing team should suffer some consequences. I've always loved the breaking water balloons as a punishment." The crew quickly started preparing a water balloon. Hae Jin said, "I think that vindictive winners should be punished also." He went over and grabbed me as Shin-dong was about to break the balloon over his head. He kissed me and we both got drenched. And so, the program ended.

Chapter 18
Concluding Remarks
Epilogue

The persons who kidnapped Park Hae Jin and Martha Karr were never caught. Mr. Park was able to resume his acting career but liked to grow his hair out white between gigs. They adopted his two biological children. The children were ages 13 and 15 when Martha died. The children were able to remember their mother in later years. She loved them so much. Mr. Park accepted a Best Actor award dressed in black with his braided white hair a year after Martha died. He was 57. Here's an interview given by her children a few years later.

The interview

Their Children Talk About Growing up with PHJ and Martha

When Hae Jin's and Martha's children were interviewed at the ages of 20 and 18 for a K-Drama in which they appeared with their father, they were asked about their mother, Martha, and what family life was like then.

"Mom always called us by nicknames which she got from her teddy bears. I'm Dawn and my brother is Ralphy."

"She was always with us it seemed even though she was working a lot. Even when she wasn't with us, somehow, she made such an impression on us that it felt as though she was there.

"She and Dad had these 'routines' they had developed to help us. When I fell down or hurt myself and started crying, she would call out to my dad, 'Mr. Park, Dawn is crying.' In would rush my dad and by the time he got there, he was crying. Then Mom would start crying all that while cleaning my injury and putting a band-aid on it. If it was on my leg, Dad would suddenly grab his leg and say, 'What about my leg, Martha? Mom would push up his pant leg, disinfect the spot, and put a band-aid on it. Mom would give it a kiss and say, 'It's all better now, don't cry.' He would exclaim, 'But you didn't give Dawn a kiss on her leg!' 'You're right, Hae Jin! Maybe you should kiss it.' He would kiss my leg and say, 'It's all better now, don't cry. Now it's time to wipe our tears away and smile.' And we would."

Ralphy said, "One time Mom caught Dawn and me arguing and cursing each other out with some bad words. Mom yelled out, 'Hae Jin, get your butt in here! Your kids are busy cussing up a storm!' Dad came in and said, 'Who the fuck did you say these kids are? I say they're your kids.'

"Mom said, 'I'm not putting up with this shit, you know damn well they're our kids. I guess we'll have to start talking like this when we're on TV or out at a fucking restaurant since our kids seem to think that it's so cool! Or maybe when their friends come over, I could just say, 'What the fuck would you guys like for a snack?' Both Dawn and I yelled, 'No!!

"Mom and Dad then just left saying, 'Fuck this damn shit!'"

"We played so many board and card games. We played a game that Dawn and I thought every family played. But it turned out that none of our friends had ever even heard of it.

"It's called pinochle. Mom brought it from the old country -America."

Dawn joined back in, "Although Mom and Dad were affectionate around us, they weren't overly so. They always kept their bedroom door locked and seemed to spend a lot of time in there. They took 'nap breaks' there. One time when I was about 12, I came into the living room late at night and found them making out. She was sitting on his lap. His arms were around her, literally crushing her to him. They broke apart when they heard me. Mom then told me this story while they held each other's hands.

"Dawn, I believe, a long time ago in the universe, a double star was broken apart. The two-star pieces were flung far away in different directions. These two pieces of the star gradually became smaller over millions and billions of years as they looked for each other. Finally, strangely, and seemingly accidentally, they fell through the sky to the exact same place and met again in a difficult situation as human beings. In that situation, they each discovered their counterpart. Nowadays, we try to recreate that one star through some very big hugs. I hope you don't mind.' Then she asked, 'Do you need a drink of water? Your dad and I are heading to bed. Good night, now.' It seemed like such a weird speech, but now I think I get it."

Ralphy said, "One time when I was nine, I told Mom I liked a girl at school and how could I get her to like me back? She said, 'For each age, it's a little different. But for your age, I think acting goofy works. Girls like guys who like them so much that the boys forget their pride and do things that they think the girls will notice. Sometimes, boys just do stupid stuff on their own, either naturally or accidentally. For example, you could stand on your head or show her how fast you can run or how strong you are. But, even better, you could fall over on your headstand, trip while running, or not be able to move a heavy weight. Girls say they hate that stuff, but they actually love it. If you can catch just a little smile from her, then you can change your tactics to bring her treats or walk her home. You can be more thoughtful and gentler - more like your dad.

"Dad was always in love, with us and with Mom. He seemed amazed that we were such great kids, and that Mom was such a great person. In other words, he was a little odd and crazy. So was she, I guess, but they were happy. We were all there as she died. My dad held her hand as she said her last words to him, 'My time has ended happily because you made me happy.'"